'PHOBOS!'

BY JERRY DONALDSON AND RACHEL TANON

PITTSBURGH, PENNSYLVANIA 15238

RoseDog Books
585 Alpha Drive, Suite 103
Pittsburgh, PA 15238
Visit our website at *www.rosedogbookstore.com*

ISBN: 979-8-88925-378-5
eISBN: 979-8-88925-878-0

‘PHOBOS!’

CHAPTER 1
THE EVENT

"Sara are you still outside glued to your telescope?" the voice questioned pleasantly through the crisp air of the darkening, star-lit night.

It was her mother. Nine-year-old Sara Taylor had spent that evening, as she had on so many others, exploring the captivating delights of the nighttime sky through her Newtonian (reflector type) telescope. She had been enchanted with the stars and planets ever since her parents took her to a planetarium when she was just six years old.

This particular night had been devoted to viewing her favorite planet, Mars. Tonight should prove to be exceptional since she had learned its orbit around the sun would bring it as close to Earth as it would ever get. That's if one could call thirty million miles 'close.'

Sara had been learning all about the planets and their moons in her fourth-grade class...a subject that had captured her imagination. She'd even gone so far as to badger her father into mounting a poster of our solar system on the wall of her room, right at the foot of her bed. She'd also encouraged her mother to allow her to leave on the lava lamp that stood on her dresser as she was going to sleep. The shimmering light it cast on the poster seemed to make the planets come alive. She studied that poster every night and, in time, learned the names of each of the planets and many of their moons. Mars, the 'Red Planet,' seemed to glow with a particular brilliance in the lamp's flickering light.

The telescope, Sara's most prized possession, had been a present from her parents the year before, on her eighth birthday. As telescopes go, this was an exceptionally good one. A Celestron NexStar 8 SE. It's an eight-inch, computer operated, reflector model that was capable of revealing the planets in all of their glorious detail. She had, in her own fanciful way, chosen to name it Nexter. This might seem a bit advanced for a little girl in the fourth grade, but with her sharp mind, Sara had quickly mastered the telescope's handheld controller, allowing her to precisely focus in on the treasures the universe had to yield.

Once again her mother called out, lovingly but forcefully this time, "Sara, are you out there?"

In response, the little girl sighed impatiently at the familiar call. Obviously the decoy pillows she'd arranged on her bed hadn't quite worked.

Even though it was much past her bedtime, she knew in just a few more minutes it would be dark enough to see far more deeply into space than usual. Sara pleaded, "Oh Mom, just a few more minutes...tonight's the best night. It's the Mars Close Approach, and if you don't let me see it now, I may not be able to see it again for more than fifteen years!"

Her mother sighed and smiled, saying, "How could I argue with that? Alright, but you're going to have to make up for it tomorrow night...no exceptions."

Sara chuckled as she became 'glued,' as her mother called it, back to Nexter's eye piece. Gathering up her notebook and pen, she began recording her observations of the 'Red Planet.' It would be a composition intended for presentation to her teacher and class the next day. The close proximity of Mars made it more brilliant than ever, and after viewing for a minute or two, she pulled away to add to her notes.

Then looking back, she just barely caught sight of a streak of light...there...just to the left of Mars. The long, luminous tail was a give-away since she knew meteoroids and asteroids don't leave tails in their tracks. She had seen several of these before but never one so close to a planet. But stranger still, it seemed to be headed straight for Mars. It was a comet.

Sara thought to herself, *This is amazing! Maybe I'm actually going to see an impact!* She could hardly contain her excitement as the streak speared closer and closer to the planet. But then, at some distance short of the planet's horizon, the comet just disappeared! There was no impact at all...just darkness surrounding the glowing orb of Mars.

"Perhaps," she mused to herself, "it had just passed behind the far side of the planet and would soon appear again, streaking out to the right."

She was transfixed by sheer anticipation, and every second that passed seemed like an eternity. But in the end, after an ample amount of time had passed, nothing happened! Where had it gone? It was really there! She didn't imagine it! What could have happened? Twice more her attention was fixed on the eyepiece in hopes of getting the answer.

"I suppose," she speculated, "it could have landed on the far side of Mars. What a nasty trick!"

In total disappointment, Sara shut down the telescope and pouted her way into the house.

As she lay nestled in her bed, the curious behavior of the comet became an endless replay in her mind's eye. Following each replay came the same question, what could have happened? The real puzzle was she hadn't seen the comet meet the planet's horizon. She should have seen that, even if it had met the ground on the far side. In time, however, Sara's swelling drowsiness overcame her frustration, and she drifted into merciful sleep.

Later that night, her mother peeked in to check on her. Seeing Sara asleep, she quietly crept in and turned off the lava lamp. When she got back into the living room, she said to Sara's dad, "Sometimes I worry that she spends too much time out there. At her age, she should be playing with her friends or having sleepovers. Although, I can't complain about her grades, and she does seem to have a real curiosity for, what is it called, astrology?"

Her dad corrected, "It's astronomy, and let's just see where it goes for a while. Next year it could be something completely different."

After breakfast the next morning, Sara turned on the television in hopes of finding out if there was any news about 'her' comet. Much to her delight, one station offered a short commentary about some kind of curious activity around Mars, but no details were known yet. Even so...she thought to herself, *I think that I'd better keep what I saw between Nexter and myself, at least for now.*

That evening, as they were having dinner, Sara heard someone on television mention Mars. She practically sprang from her chair before asking if she could go listen to the news.

"Okay, our little astronomer," her mother chuckled as she and Sara's dad looked at each other, bemused.

The astronomer being interviewed explained that shortly after the comet had mysteriously disappeared, his high-powered telescope had detected an object traveling away from Mars on the opposite side. It was just a faint glow against the blackness of space and didn't exhibit the self-revealing tail of a comet. Perhaps, he speculated, the comet had impacted the surface and dislodged a large chunk of the planet that rocketed skyward. He tracked the object for a while, taking several photographs, and then turned back to observing the planet and its two moons, Phobos and Deimos.

Deimos, the smaller of the two, is composed mostly of rock, is irregularly shaped with a cratered surface, and measures fifteen miles at its widest point. It orbits far above the surface, making it easy to spot as it continues to endlessly wend its way around the fourth planet from the sun.

Oval shaped Phobos, not unlike the appearance of an oversized potato, is about twenty-seven miles long and eighteen miles across. It's made up largely of iron and rock, pockmarked with hundreds of craters, and has a very large indentation on one end named The Stickney Crater.

He wasn't alarmed when, at first, he couldn't spot Phobos because it travels in a very low orbital path and can be difficult to detect against the rust-colored surface of the planet. It traverses the entire circumference about once every eight hours, but during the four hours it should have been visible, he could not locate it. Calculations had shown that with its low, decaying orbit, it would eventually crash onto the surface of Mars, but that event wouldn't occur for another fifty million years.

It had unconsciously begun to creep into his thoughts that what he had seen trekking off to the right could actually have been Phobos itself! He desperately tried to suppress any such idea, but at the moment, there didn't seem to be any other logical explanation. So, as improbable as it seemed, he reluctantly went on to suppose that the comet could have made direct contact with Phobos, knocking the now possibly former Martian moon out of its orbit and returning it to the status of an asteroid. And since the object seemed to be in one solid piece, the comet's impact must have been perfectly inelastic. That is, it didn't break up Phobos on contact but just added its energy and mass to it, propelling it off on some unknown journey into space.

Not being entirely comfortable with this wild conclusion, he wasn't yet ready to reveal it. So he ended the broadcast interview by saying, "Continuing observation over the next few days will yield more detailed information."

Sara bristled with excitement. She had seen it. Little nine-year-old Sara had witnessed the same thing as the world's astronomers. "Eureka!" she shrieked as she ran back to the dinner table, where she could barely get her words out fast enough. Her mom and dad looked at her with pride when little Sara finished her story with the announcement, "I knew I was meant to be a scientist one day, guys!"

Soon observatories around the world confirmed Phobos could no longer be found in orbit. Their telescopes, now re-programmed to track the more than curious object eventually revealed it was the wayward ex-moon.

Early tracking calculations suggested it might be doomed to travel throughout the vast universe forever. But within weeks of that published speculation, further plotting suggested other possible fates. One being recaptured in the Main Asteroid Belt, its suspected place of origin. The asteroid belt is a region in the solar system between Jupiter and Mars that contains possibly billions of solid, irregularly shaped bodies called asteroids or minor planets. Others had it crashing to its demise into one of the other planets in our solar system. The least probable, but still to be considered, was the possibility it could somehow return to visit us far off in the future.

For the first few years, people the world over followed the updates of Phobos's flight path, eagerly waiting to see if any of these predictions would be confirmed. Eventually this escaping asteroid dimmed from the sight of all but the most powerful telescopes. The world's speculations and concerns about when and if it might return someday, much like Halley's Comet, faded from public interest. There were, of course, occasional specials on television regarding Phobos, largely based on the latest calculations, but its ultimate fate remained an unsolved mystery.

For Sara, this incident only served to heighten her already overflowing fascination with astronomy. It would continue to be her main interest far beyond her grammar school days.

CHAPTER 2

AMY

Sara managed good grades throughout grammar school despite spending much of her spare time with the stars, leaving little room for study and homework. To her, the diploma she received at graduation was just a passport for the next journey toward her goal of becoming an astronomer.

She had always looked forward to summers, with no homework, no commitments—other than household chores—and no distractions, allowing for maximum time to partake in the pastime that captivated her. Her parents had always been tolerant of her single-mindedness but that summer they had rented a cottage on a local lake for a two-week vacation. It would mean two weeks without Nexter, but Sara thought it might be good to take a little break and get a fresh start in the fall. After all, she would be going into high school and was beginning to get a new perspective on everything.

She didn't quite know what she was going to do at the lake because she had never been much for socializing. She had summoned up the discipline to leave her astronomy books at home, so after breakfast she would wander down to the beach and just people watch for a while.

On the third morning of this pastime, two girls about her age came over, introduced themselves, and asked her name. Sara, somewhat of an introvert due to the reclusive nature of telescope watching, was kind of caught off guard. She didn't have any really close friends and these girls were total strangers.

Yet with her new attitude, she found it quite easy to say, "Hi my name is Sara. Are you here on vacation?"

That kicked off the usual round of get-acquainted questions and answers.

They struck up a friendship and spent several long days just being teenagers at the beach. They talked about things like clothes, makeup, future dreams, and, of course, boys. Sara's entire experience with boys had been limited to a couple of simple flirtations in the later years of grammar school. Her preoccupation with Nexter and science didn't leave much time for, or interest in, that kind of involvement. It was fascinating, however, to hear how they compared one boy to another and how they wished certain boys would ask them out. She didn't bring up her interest in astronomy, knowing it bored most people her age. The vacation ended with goodbyes and promises to keep in touch, which would never be kept.

During the drive home, Sara stared out the car window wondering if she might be missing out on something with her dedication to science. The reunion with Nexter put all thoughts on that subject aside for now. A few more weeks of summer and it was off to high school, where she was to have her first encounter with Amy.

Amy Bradford was Sara's polar opposite. Where Sara's focus was academic, Amy's was social.

Sara was a very analytical person. She didn't beat around the bush. If her friends were having problems, then Sara was the first to offer a solution, being as direct and matter-of-fact as possible. "It doesn't matter what he thinks. You're in three honors courses and you need as little distractions as possible. We have a huge project coming due. You don't have time for dating anyways," Sara counseled one of the girls before class.

This drove Amy crazy. "Can't you see she's upset? We get it Sara. You're a nerd who only cares about one thing. But the rest of us are entitled to a life." Amy turned to the girl. "Come on. Let's go to the locker room before class starts and fix your makeup."

Sara stood there, red faced, as the two girls walked away. She thought to herself, *She always does this! I'm just being logical. She's focused on the wrong things.*

Unfortunately for the two girls, they shared several classes together. It seemed no matter what Sara did, she could not get away from Amy. They challenged each other in each class, debating the class subject matter until the teacher forced them to move on with the lesson. It seemed nothing could bring them together. They liked different music, different clothes, different subjects, different everything...except for soccer.

Sara found the sport exhilarating. The physical workout the games provided made a perfect counterweight to the sedentary nature of stargazing. Her skills and passion for the game developed so quickly that when the soccer coach noticed her playing in pick-up games around the campus, he recruited her to play on the varsity team even though she was still a freshman.

When Sara showed up for her first practice, her jaw dropped. There, in a one-on-one scrimmage being cheered on by her teammates, was Amy. It took everything Sara had not to turn around and leave. She griped to herself, "First she's in many of my classes and now here, too? When will it end?"

But forcing herself to focus on how impressive extracurricular activities look on a university application, Sara walked over to the other players with her head held high. Amy saw her coming and their eyes locked. Next thing you know, Amy is sprinting toward the ball. She flipped around the other player, stole the ball, and made a goal so quickly the whole team was so amazed they all started to cheer. Sara was impressed but wouldn't let it show. Amy jogged by, smirking at Sara as she passed.

Neither of them ever expected to become friends. However, their chemistry on the field was undeniable. They worked together almost effortlessly, each one's style on the field complementing the other's perfectly. Sara and Amy were always positioned near one another during games. The coaches saw how, together, they brought up the entire team.

During the season, they somewhat warmed up to each other, but completely flipping your opinion about somebody you have never cared for seldom happens. If these two were going to bond off the playing field, their feelings had to be genuine and the commitment absolute. You can't cement a bond like that with words. It takes that special eye-to-eye gaze, looking directly into each other's souls.

It came for them while reluctantly complementing each other after a particularly good game when they both just went silent and held that stare for many seconds. Sara broke the spell with, "Maybe there's a chance for you and me to be friends after all." Amy hesitated, not wanting to admit she was thinking the same thing. As much as they had despised each other they both had to admit to themselves they had come to admire some qualities of the other.

Amy looked away in thought, then looked back at Sara and said, "Alright, where do we go from here?" Sara said, "How about the locker room?"

That was it. They walked off the field together.

By the middle of the season, these once bitter enemies were inseparable. They were at each other's side for every class, and they'd even made plans to go to college together.

It was Amy's dream to get into administration at some university. She had little interest in any of the sciences but nonetheless enjoyed spending hours with her friend at the telescope, listening to her ramble on about planets and moons and comets and meteors. But even so, it was not beyond Amy to sometimes remark, "Sara, what a nerd you are."

In most things, nonetheless, they were truly two facets of the same personality. They pushed each other to do better and were always planning for the future. But still, much of their time together was spent acting like kids. Trips out to do grocery shopping, for example, might collapse into finding the best snack shop in town. Despite their beginnings, they couldn't imagine a better friendship.

Amy came to love that Sara knew exactly what she wanted. On her birthday, Amy had the team bring Sara balloons decorated to look like planets or moons. At school, Amy would press her to help with her science homework, in part because she understood her passion for the subject but also because she was always assured of getting the highest grade with Sara's help.

Yet, even with all this new activity and unfamiliar attention, everything still fell secondary to Sara's passion for astronomy. So whenever a night game was to be played, Sara was almost always mysteriously ill, particularly when the skies were exceptionally clear. On those occasions, Amy knew quite well that she could always find her fixed to her beloved telescope. And on those nights when Amy was dancing the night away with whichever boy she was dating, Sara's date would still be Nexter.

CHAPTER 3
MR. NICHOLS

Sara did well enough with her freshman courses but none of them were really aimed at someone with her long-term ambition. The soccer team had won their division but lost in the city finals.

During that summer there were some pick-up games at the local park, but times when there wasn't a game, Sara and Amy seemed to be joined at the hip. They were always together at each other's homes, out jogging, or finding some mischief to get into. Sara would sometimes drag Amy to the planetarium and name all the simulated stars and planets projected onto the ceiling. They were teenagers, so of course there were dates, but nothing serious or long-lasting.

Overall it was just a lazy summer, and Sara's compulsion for everything science seemed to have been somewhat tempered by her friendship with Amy. Summer ended and a few weeks into tenth grade, a single incident lit that fire up again.

It was a bit unnerving at first when her tenth-grade science teacher, Mr. Nichols, asked her to remain after class. Her first thoughts were, *Now what did I do?* Perhaps it'd been a mistake for her to ask all those many questions...though the rest of the class found it a relief when she could so easily stall the lesson. Yet Mr. Nichols was Sara's favorite teacher, and she'd thought it a great misfortune they'd never chatted before one-on-one. Even so, she'd always sensed he was the real deal—her greatest instructor.

No matter what questions she'd put to him during class, he'd always come back with truly meaningful answers. These many rewards to her curiosity, however, had always encouraged her to continue the practice. Sometimes, perhaps, just to see if, maybe just one time, there'll be a question he couldn't answer. But it had never happened.

On this specific afternoon, after detaining Sara and all of her other classmates had left, Mr. Nichols approached her desk encompassed by an aura, both stern and excited. *Now I'm in for it*, she thought to herself, with no idea of what to expect.

After a short pause, he finally asked, "How do you know so much about the solar system, young lady?" In the question, the man had taken great care to suppress his eagerness, and that question was completely unexpected by the youngster.

Her immediate thought was, *Here's someone who doesn't think I'm a nerd but might actually be interested in my passion.* Sara virtually exploded with enthusiasm as she told of her long fascination with astronomy, of the chart of the solar system that had graced her bedroom wall for years, of the countless nights she'd spent with Nexter, and the books she'd devoured. To the delight of Mr. Nichols, it all poured out as Sara basked in the exhilaration she felt at her favorite teacher's profound interest in her enthusiasm for the subject.

She went on to recount, "When I was six, Mom and Dad took me to a planetarium. From the first moment I saw the display of stars, planets, and moons projected onto the ceiling, I knew that I had to have my own telescope so I could see the real starry wonders themselves. For two years I begged my parents, and then finally, on my eighth birthday, I unwrapped my wonderful Nexter.

"It was the most wonderful moment of my life! Ever since then, I've dreamed of becoming a real astronomer. Then, when I was in the fourth grade, I knew it was truly meant to be, and I felt it in my bones when I actually saw that comet pass behind Mars." She chuckled at the memory of that thrilling moment. "I still remember being so mad when I didn't see an impact. Now look at all the excitement over Phobos. It's traveling right through our solar system!"

Mr. Nichols skillfully contained his excitement on hearing that little Sara had actually witnessed the event for herself. Then suddenly she realized how animated she had become and shrank a bit. Modestly, she responded to question after question about what she'd actually witnessed. But when he finally recognized her obvious discomfort, he drew back a bit and apologized.

After a few moments pause, to reflect on the discovery of an actual eyewitness to one of the most wonderful events of the age, he comforted Sara with the comment, "It's amazing to meet someone who's actually seen it! It all happened so fast that you are one of only a handful of people the world over who actually saw it happen live! What incredibly good fortune. I can see how you could have interpreted it as an omen."

Then, in a most thoughtful pose, Mr. Nichols turned on his heels and began to stroke his chin. For the next few minutes he paced slowly back and forth in front of his student and then said, "I have to tell you," he began, "that before coming here, I spent almost thirty years with NASA as an astronomical physicist. After early retirement, I took this teaching job in the hope that in such a pool of students I might find one with a passion for outer space. A hungry young mind that I might tutor and mentor and steer toward my passion for astrophysics."

Sara sat, mouth agape and wide-eyed with amazement. This finally explained the depth and range of the knowledge of astronomy which he'd so easily displayed.

"I've never before," he continued, "had a student who asked so many questions and questions of such advanced interest as you. You've no idea how refreshing it is to see someone show the same kind of curiosity in the universe as I have. Maybe you'd like me to talk to your parents about some private tutoring, perhaps?"

Sara's level of astonishment swelled even higher, if that was possible. Then, taking a few seconds to compose herself, she replied, "That'd be wonderful. I'll ask my parents!" After another slight pause to complete her recovery, she rose to her feet, preparing to leave. And then, "Oh yes," she chirped, "there's just one more question I'd like to ask before I leave."

A broad grin spread across the teacher's face as he clucked in reply, "Fire away!"

In a slightly sheepish tone, Sara went on, "I have always wondered why the impact of the comet didn't smash Phobos into little pieces?"

His reply began, "Ah, that might be your toughest question yet. One could guess, as is already suspected, that the former Martian moon had possibly originated in the main Asteroid Belt. As you know, the belt is made up of billions of asteroids of every size, from pebbles to almost planet-size boulders, which very often maimpact with each other, resembling balls on a pool table. All of the craters on Phobos are clear indicators in support of this theory. And if this idea is correct, and if all of those impacts hadn't already destroyed Phobos, it would be unlikely that a small comet alone could have done much damage.

"I'm sure you are aware that there are a couple of theories about Phobos's actual makeup. One says it's made of a solid chunk of rock, and another that it's a porous body that's somewhat hollow. Also the really big impact that created the Stickney Crater might very well have been what knocked it out of the belt. Such an impact could have compacted and hardened the sides and bottom of the crater, making those surfaces very resilient. Similar to the tempering of metals.

"Furthermore, figuring the comet's path while approaching Mars and the position of Phobos at the moment of impact, it may very well have struck right in that crater, a perfect pre-made divot. I know there are several suppositions about its future, but the most intriguing one to me is that it could, by some 'trick of physics,' return to our neck of the woods someday. Of course some of this is just speculation on my part."

Sara, quite satisfied with his answer, said her thanks and just kind of floated out the door. She fantasized all the way home about her future possibilities.

That evening, Sara, with no way to disguise her eagerness, told her parents about what had happened after class that day, and how Mr. Nichols wanted to talk with them about tutoring her in the science of astronomy. In an obviously desirous tone, she went on to suggest how such tutelage would help her realize her now burning ambition.

Mom and Dad both listened intently before Dad finally remarked, "Maybe that telescope will be worth what we paid for it after all."

They arranged to meet with Mr. Nichols later in the week. At the meeting, he explained that as a dedicated instructor, he'd always been on the lookout for students who showed an exceptional interest in the solar system and what a pleasant surprise it was finding someone with Sara's obvious potential. He suggested he could help her construct a strong curriculum for her high school education and for college as well. But that wasn't the only way that he might help.

He continued, "I'm truly amazed that a fourteen-year-old should be so engrossed in this field and so hopeful to be a part of the scientific world. That kind of enthusiasm should always be energetically encouraged. And since I've previously had a professional career at NASA for almost three decades, I could even imagine helping little Sara here, one day apply for entrance into the United States Space Program, and who knows, even as a potential astronaut."

Sara had never thought about actually going into space herself, but even at first thought, the idea was truly fascinating! To be able to explore the mysteries of space first-hand, how could she not love that idea?

Sara's dad pondered over Mr. Nichols's suggestions for several moments as she looked up to him, hopefully. He finally commented, "It all sounds fine to me, depending on the cost of course."

Mr. Nichols grinned knowingly as he responded, "Don't be concerned about that. Teaching is my passion, particularly in the case of a youngster as sharp as Sara."

Dad nodded his appreciation and said, "It's settled then. But, little lady, you know that you're setting yourself up for many years of hard work. Make sure this is truly what you want so you're not just wasting this gentleman's time."

Sara, with bouncing excitement, just grinned broadly. The game was truly on!

In the days and weeks that followed, Sara grew from being an average student into one of excellence now that she was working towards a real goal instead of just daydreaming about what could be.

Amy's efforts at getting her a steady boyfriend would be futile now because she was just too busy for any kind of serious relationship. So it was while her friends were out dating or frolicking at parties, Sara spent her nighttime hours star gazing and her days hunting bookstores and libraries for publications on astronomy and physics. Much of her spare time was spent scanning such volumes and filling notebooks in a most organized manner with all sorts of facts and figures on these subjects.

CHAPTER 4
RYAN

Knowing of Sara's drive to consume as much as she could about astrology, Mr. Nichols's tutoring didn't require her to do much extracurricular work during her high school years. He, of course, was always there to answer questions and supply what little encouragement she might need.

Throughout high school, she didn't have her nose to the 'scientific grindstone' all the time. She attended sporting events, parties, various other social events, and of course continued to play soccer.

Come senior year, Mr. Nichols assisted Sara with her selection of a university that offered the best schooling for an astronomical career. Her one steadfast requirement was it had to be a university that Amy could attend as well. Ultimately, her persistence paid off.

College proved to be a fun time for Sara and Amy. They were glad to have a couple of classes together but disappointed when there weren't any double rooms available in the dorm. They settled for a small, two-bedroom apartment just off the campus grounds. It would become their home for the next four years.

Even with her scholarships, grants, and her parents' help, Sara still had to get a part time job for books and living expenses, which would be split with Amy. She naturally applied at the planetarium, but nothing was available. She ended up getting a job as a waitress at Outback. Not very fitting for a future scientist.

Amy snared a boyfriend during the first year and was still trying to pair Sara up with some boy so they could, at least, double date. Yet, even with such a social life available, Sara had more interest in visiting with Mom and Dad whenever possible, perhaps with an ulterior motive in the opportunity it provided her to companion with Nexter. That was, until she met Ryan.

Ryan Arness and his older brother, Randy, had grown up products of a stable family life, right here in the same town as the university. They were three years apart and, like most brothers, seemed to always be fighting, and then five minutes later would be back playing together again.

Randy showed a talent for music at an early age. After college he went to the Julliard School of Music for a short time, and then came back and built a career writing musical scores for movies and plays. Ryan, on the other hand, couldn't play a note but discovered an affinity for math in the fourth grade. In all the other subjects he was, at best, a B- student, but it was a rare math test he couldn't 'ace.'

First year in high school, the school counselor, aware of his skill in math but lack of good grades in other subjects, suggested he concentrate on physics saying, "It might open some career doors."

Ryan had hoped to get accepted at a university, but that comment from the counselor made him realize his grades just weren't good enough. At the end of the school year, he signed up for summer school, planning to retake some finals in the fall. When Randy heard about this, he said, "Yeah, well with your history, you're probably just wasting the summer, little brother."

If Ryan needed a challenge that was it.

Summer school didn't turn out to be the drudgery he had feared. Luckily he could skip the math part, and a lot of the rest was review and left for study at home. In the fall he was allowed to retake most of his finals and raised his grade from a B- to an A. He received a certificate of completion showing his grade, which he immediately waved in front of Randy's face.

During sophomore year, his grades improved. Physics became his passion, and getting into a university was a little closer to becoming a reality. Even so, he certainly wasn't a math nerd, having a full social life and competing on the swimming and soccer teams. He maintained those good grades right through senior year, ending up with a good enough grade point average to get accepted at the local university. His first day in the university physics class, he didn't even notice the girl sitting right behind him. It was Sara.

Not seeking any kind of relationship, Sara still took note of the tall, well-dressed student sitting in front of her. He didn't ask a lot of questions yet seemed totally at ease with all the physics being thrown at them. It didn't take long for her to realize he was, by far, the best student in the class. Physics didn't come easy for her, so she thought, *Maybe he could be the help I need with this class.*

She gathered up enough courage to approach him after class one day and said, "Excuse me. My name is Sara, and I sit right behind you in physics. I was wondering if you ever did any tutoring?"

He said, "Well Sara who sits behind me, I'm Ryan, and I've never thought about it. What do you have in mind?"

Sara explained, "I'm majoring in astronomy and can't get there without physics, but it's always been a struggle for me. It took up a lot of my study time during high school, and now I'm having a really tough time with all these new concepts."

He said, "This is quite a coincidence. I'm majoring in planetary geology, so both our aspirations lie somewhere up in the cosmos. As for tutoring, weekdays are out. I work at Barnes and Noble on Saturdays, and I usually save Sundays for more study."

A disappointed Sara said, "I understand. Thanks anyway."

He said, "Wait a minute. Maybe there's a way I could study and tutor at the same time. We could get together for a while on Sunday afternoons and review that week's material. It would be like studying together. Would that work for you?"

A hopeful Sara said, "That sounds perfect, and I would be glad to pay you for your time."

Ryan smiled and said, "What? I couldn't charge a fellow scientist for a little help."

They agreed on the local Starbucks as their off-campus classroom. With that decided, they said goodbye, and as Sara walked away, he admitted, "Incidentally, I definitely knew you were sitting behind me."

Sara quickly turned away not wanting him to see the blush on her face.

The following Sunday afternoon, they had their first session in a booth way in the back, not wanting to disturb the other customers. Ryan volunteered to get coffee, but Sara demanded, "Nope, I'll take care of that."

While drinking that coffee, he asked enough questions to get an idea of what to focus on. The next hour or so he went over those items until she said, "I've got it."

After that first meeting, Sara thought to herself, *He's got a great personality, and what a natural tutor, at least for me.*

From then on, they would meet after every physics class for a couple of minutes to decide if that day's lesson would require another session.

The first few of these tutorials were all business, but little by little, interests other than physics began to casually slip into their conversation. It wasn't anything too personal, just some off topic comments that might elicit a laugh or maybe a discussion about a particular book or television program.

Then, in the middle of one afternoon, Ryan suddenly closed his book, leaned forward, fixed his gaze directly into hers, and asked, "How would you like to knock off and go to a movie or something?"

Sara's face lit up as she replied, without hesitation, "Sounds great to me!"

They settled on a movie and went there together in Ryan's car. It was a pleasant, physics free afternoon, and on the drive back, they talked about the movie, and Ryan asked if she thought they needed to complete today's discussion. Sara was tempted to say yes, but it was getting late, and her laundry was piling up back in the apartment.

When he dropped her off by her car, Ryan said, "That was definitely a lot nicer than sitting in a booth at Starbucks all afternoon. Maybe we can find a better place for our next get together. See you in class tomorrow."

During her drive home, Sara had an unfamiliar feeling about the day's events. She tried to tell herself it wasn't Ryan, and the movie wasn't a date, just an outing with a friend. Back in the apartment, just the mention of a movie with Ryan had Amy prying, "So where's this going?"

Sara tried to turn her off with, "It's not going anywhere. It was just a movie, that's all. I shouldn't have told you."

Next time Sara indicated she could use some tutoring, Ryan suggested, "How about if we just go sit on one of the benches outside and go over today's lecture while it's still fresh?"

Sara said, "I have another class right now, but could we do it at four o'clock?"

He said, "Okay, I'll meet you back here."

It was a short walk down the path between campus buildings to the first bench where they settled down, opened their books, and started to go over that day's material. After covering what she was unsure about, Ryan casually turned the conversation to how compatible they seemed to be and how they were on similar paths in life. Then, a skittery and nervous Ryan leaned in very close to her with a longing look in his eyes. Sara, suspecting what was about to happen, felt somewhat uncomfortable and excited at the same time.

They both went silent, stared into each other's eyes, and closed the distance between them until their lips met. Sensing Ryan was going to pull away after a short time, Sara put her arms around him and held him close. They separated with that awkward feeling that often accompanies a first kiss and agreed it was time to get going. They walked back down the path in an uneasy silence, neither one wanting to express their feelings just yet. When they parted, there was another moment of silence when it seemed like it would happen again. It didn't.

The minute Amy walked into the apartment, Sara challenged her with, "You'll never guess what happened today."

Amy pursed her lips, contemplated for a few seconds, and said, "Hmm, you failed a science test."

A somewhat irritated Sara said, "Come on be serious."

Amy tried again, "Ryan's not going to tutor you anymore."

Sara was way too excited to play this game anymore, so gushed out, "Just the opposite. Ryan kissed me."

Amy shrieked, "Whoo this is big. Where did this happen?"

Sara explained, "Ryan suggested we go sit on a campus bench instead of going to Starbucks and it just happened."

"What do you mean 'it just happened?' Details, details!" demanded Amy.

Sara said, "Alright, we were talking, and he leaned toward me, and I have to admit I leaned a little myself, and we just kissed. I'm almost embarrassed to say that I wouldn't let him pull away."

"So you liked it. Sara the science nerd is having a relationship with something, or someone in this case, besides, what do you call it? Nexter?"

"I don't know about a relationship. It was just one kiss," Sara said, unconvincingly.

"So," Amy teased, "are you going to see him again? Is he going to call you?"

"Don't joke. I've been kissed before, but it never made me feel like this," Sara confessed.

Ryan called later that evening, and after the hellos said, "Look, about that kiss today. If it was out of line, I apologize. It's just that I really like being around you, and I'm hoping you don't see us as just tutor and student."

This is the kind of thing Sara had no problem rejecting in the past, but with these new, strange feelings, she heard herself say, "No, everything today was okay...I-I mean it was fine."

With a sigh of relief, Ryan said, "Great. I just wanted to make sure it wouldn't cause any problems between us."

"No, there's no problem," Sara said.

"Good, so I'll see you in class tomorrow, and maybe we can go to lunch after," he suggested.

"Yeah, that sounds good," Sara said, trying not to show her excitement.

When they ended the call, Amy immediately asked, "What was that all about?"

"Oh Ryan was just concerned about what happened today, and we're going to have lunch tomorrow."

Amy kidded, "Well maybe you're finally going to have some romance in your life instead of all that science stuff."

That lunch was the first of many to follow, along with long, pleasant strolls around the campus grounds, which could drift into hours. They were definitely heading in the direction of a serious relationship. It was like passing into a phase of life that seemed almost predestined. There was no question about it, Sara was falling in love.

It was on one of those walks Ryan told Sara a story about when at age fourteen on a camping trip with his parents, he found a small black rock. It somehow intrigued him, so he took it home and then to his ninth-grade science teacher who, after an investigation with the class microscope, said he thought it was a meteorite. He suggested Ryan take it to the local science museum for further clarification. Sure enough, they verified it as a meteorite, and that simple event sparked his interest in planetary geometry.

He had, over the years, accumulated an impressive collection of meteoric rocks from sources like flea markets, online sites, and many field trips around the country. Given his enthusiasm while relating his story, Sara realized the passion he felt for his field equaled what she felt for astronomy. One more reason, she thought, to believe this relationship was meant to be. She'd discovered someone who shared the same dreams. As time passed they found the decisions they made, alone or in unison, seemed uncannily prone to join their lives together. Their companionship seemed to radiate an aura that was clearly noticeable to everyone around them.

Occasionally, when they could both get away from schoolwork and jobs, they would drive the half hour to Sara's parents' house to gaze at the skies through her telescope. She told him about Nexter, the comet, and Mr. Nichols's suggestion that she become an astronaut. Ryan, listening intently, thought it was a great idea and hinted maybe they could accomplish it together. They also began to spend a lot of time with Amy and her boyfriend. So, much to Amy's delight, she finally got her double dates. The only downside was Sara and Ryan were always talking about science stuff or, as Amy called it, 'nerd talk.'

CHAPTER 5
THE CAPTAIN'S INN

Theirs was the usual college grind of daytime classes, part-time jobs, and hours of study, which didn't leave much personal time. Yet she and Ryan somehow found time to be together. It was convenient for them Ryan was living in the dorm even though his parents lived just a few miles from the university. They made it a point to occasionally drive over and visit them.

With a campus in the area, there were more than the usual number of fast-food joints, sandwich shops, and even a few upscale restaurants. There is a coffee shop called The School Grounds and a steak house called First Degree Steaks, but their favorite restaurant is back in Sara's hometown. It's a large, century old Victorian mansion originally built by a ship's captain, now appropriately named The Captain's Inn.

Even though now serving as a restaurant, it had been meticulously kept in its original condition. It stood majestically on a sizable lot at the corner of two small streets that still showed signs of once being made of cobblestones. There's a 'widow's watch' on the roof above the second floor, recalling a time when a ship's captain would be at sea for months or even years at a time. The downstairs has a large parlor and an even larger living room that are now both furnished with intimate dining tables. The living room has a large open fireplace that, in the past, probably served as a hearth. It was in this living room that Sara and Ryan would always pick a corner table that had windows on both adjacent walls. With wintertime snow blanketing the outside grounds, these windows provided a spectacular scene.

Tuition and living expenses didn't leave much spending money, but they allowed themselves the luxury of a once-a-month, dress up dinner at this warm, inviting place. In time they became recognized regulars, always receiving a family-like welcome from the owner and the waiters. Saturday evening was reserved for this extravagance, and it was always kept just between the two of them. Halfway through their senior year, one such Saturday would become an evening they would both cherish forever.

Ryan had called the maître d' ahead of time to reserve 'their' table. It was a cold, snowy weekend, so the heat from the fireplace would be welcome and the view out the windows was certain to add some drama. On arrival, the maître d' ushered them to 'that' table. As usual, the owner came out from the kitchen to greet them, and Dale, one of their regular waiters, came over, bade them good evening, and asked if they needed to see the menu. It was a standard line used on them by most of the waiters that always produced contrived smiles.

Ryan, unusually quiet during dinner, waited until they were both finished to lean forward and fix his gaze directly into hers, more earnestly than, when at Starbucks, he first got up the courage to ask her to a movie. After nervously fumbling for something in his jacket pocket, he took her hand in his and began, "Sara, as you know before college, my preoccupation was searching for cosmic rejects. When I started here, I figured all outside activities would have to be shelved for the next four years. You've managed to put a gigantic dent in that theory."

Sara took a breath, starting to be concerned about where this was going.

He continued, "Now that we're getting close to graduation, I can tell you that the one outside activity I couldn't and don't ever want to give up is you." He opened the small box retrieved from his jacket, revealing the ring he hoped she would accept. He slipped out of his chair onto one knee and, as sincerely as his shaky voice would allow, got out the words, "Sara Taylor, will you marry me?"

It was a heart-stopping moment for Sara, and for an instant, it was like a curtain had been drawn down over her eyes. When it faded, her view of the room had shrunk down to a small spot containing only Ryan and the ring box. She thought she had instantly said yes but couldn't remember hearing those words come out of her mouth. When a bit of her composure returned, she managed a weak, "Yes," followed by a much more robust, "OH, RYAN, YES!"

When he took out the ring and slipped it onto her finger, she sank back into her chair with a warm, sweet feeling but still in somewhat of a daze. When she finally awoke to what was actually happening, she lunged out of her chair into Ryan's awaiting hug. The waiters, aware of what was going on, gathered around to applaud. The owner came out, congratulated them, and said he would be honored if they would consider his place for their reception.

They sat there for the next hour reminiscing about how they had gotten to this point and planning their future. They agreed that the wedding would have to wait until after graduation but not too long after. Sara couldn't keep from raising her left hand every few minutes to admire the ring. To her it shone brighter than any star she had ever observed. Their only other decision that night was that the wedding would take place in the church that Sara and her parents attended.

It was after midnight when an elated Ryan reluctantly dropped Sara off at her apartment. She was walking on air as she approached Amy's bedroom door and knocked. No response called for an even harder knock. A groggy sounding Amy demanded, "Sara is that you?"

"Yes. Get up. I have some awesome news," Sara ordered.

Amy shot back, "This better be good," as she staggered out the door.

When Sara told her about Ryan's proposal and her acceptance, Amy screeched, and they hugged and danced around the room for several minutes. Then Amy demanded, "Okay give...where did this happen...how did he ask you...what did you say...I want to know everything!"

As Sara was recounting every detail, she got the same thrill as she did when it was actually happening. When she was done, Amy sighed and said, "It's like a romance novel." Adding, "Well now you don't need a telescope to be starry eyed."

Sara asked, "Will you be my maid of honor?"

Amy, looking somewhat annoyed, responded, "Did you even have to ask?"

When they started to talk about things like who would be in the wedding party, what kind of gowns they would wear, etc., it became obvious it was going to be a long, sleepless night.

Ryan, anxious to tell his parents, realized it was too late to call them. Back in the dorm, his roommate, Chuck, was asleep, so he had to be content just remembering how perfectly the evening had gone. The fantasy he'd had for several years was coming true. As he lay in bed, he kept recalling every detail of his proposal and Sara's acceptance over and over. Just before sleep finally released him from this continual rerun, he decided to ask Randy to be his best man.

Having been busy with college, they had never talked about marriage or looked too far into the future. Now with just one semester remaining and no doubt they were both going to graduate, the only problem would be keeping their upcoming marriage in the back of their minds during class. Of course all her friends and classmates noticed Sara's ring and the new skip in her step. There were constant congratulations and requests for details. Sara reveled in showing off the ring and talking about Ryan.

Spring came along with final exams, celebrations about passing, and the upcoming graduation, all bringing them closer to their wedding day. Graduation was held at an amphitheater on the university grounds, where almost a hundred students got to relocate the tassel on their mortarboard caps from right to left. Later they all took part in the tradition of throwing those caps in the air. Ryan's parents held a get together attended by Sara and her parents and, of course, Amy.

CHAPTER 6

THE WEDDING

This round of college was over, but Sara and Amy would stay in the apartment until after the wedding. Ryan moved back in with his parents for now but kept his job at Barnes and Noble. Amy would help with the wedding, move back home, and take the rest of the summer off. She would be back in the fall to live in the dorm and start a Doctor of Education (EdD) program. After the honeymoon, Ryan and Sara would move into the apartment.

Weddings can be simple and quick or a big production. They were planning something in between. Even so, the 'to do' list was quite long. Their parents had gotten to know each other and agreed to share the costs, and they, along with Amy, would pitch in with all the preparation. Still, the bulk of the decisions fell to Ryan and Sara. To them it was a labor of love but a labor still.

One afternoon while driving to the Taylors' church to speak to the pastor, Sara was rattling off suggestions where they might spend their weeklong honeymoon. Ryan interrupted with, "Well we can't afford many of those, but I do have some ideas. Want to hear one?"

Sara quipped, "Sure. Aren't we're in this together?"

Ryan's first offering was, "How about someplace like Daytona Beach, Florida? It has great hotels right on the beach, it's the home of the Embry-Riddle Aeronautical University, there's lots of water sports, ocean trips, and it's just a few miles north of Cape Canaveral."

An impressed Sara said, "A wedding, a day at the beach, and a visit to Cape Canaveral! Any more ideas you have can just be filed away."

After they spoke with the pastor, the church was reserved, and a June date picked. The guest list, always a struggle between the number of guests and the cost, was simplified by selecting The Captain's Inn for the reception. The parlor would work perfectly as a dance floor, and the dining room had a limited number of tables. Sara was going be a June bride.

Amy proved to be a perfect bride's maid, catering to Sara's every request and need. Before long, the wedding party was picked, invitations sent out, gowns selected, fittings completed, and rehearsals held. Even though things were moving along, it couldn't come soon enough for Ryan and Sara.

The wedding day arrived with a shower of light rain...the sun occasionally peeking through intermittent clouds. At seven A.M., the alarm rang in Sara's bedroom at her parents' house, waking Amy. She and Sara had been up late into the night going over everything that could go right or wrong. Even so, she couldn't believe Sara could sleep through the alarm on this, the most special of days. She thought, *I'll fix this.* and threw her pillow onto Sara's bed.

That only elicited a slight stir from Sara.

Amy yelled, "Hey, wake up! It's your wedding day!"

That did it. Sara opened her eyes and said, "Oh good morning...I was having this dream that I was standing on some far away planet. Think it means anything?"

Amy scolded, "Come on, space cadet, we have to get up and get going."

Sara's mother knocked, poked her head in, and said, "Glad to see you two are awake. Breakfast is ready downstairs."

Sara sat up, looked out the window, and, seeing raindrops amidst beams of sunlight, commented, "Well, maybe there'll at least be a rainbow."

The usual horseplay and banter between them continued as they romped down the stairs, still in their pajamas. Her dad, sitting at the kitchen table warned, "We'll be leaving here in about two hours, so I hope that's enough time for you girls to get ready."

Sara's wedding dress and Amy's gown had been stashed in a room off the vestibule at the church, so showers, hair, and makeup were all they planned to get done at home. Back upstairs, they competed for bathroom and vanity mirror time but still helped each other as much as they could. Yet they were still primping when her dad called up, "Time to go, girls."

It was nearly nine fifteen when Sara's dad dropped them off in front of the church. The photographer, tucked into a small alcove out of the rain, started snapping pictures as they were getting out of the car and continued right on into the 'get ready' room. It was a room normally used for choir practice, so it would be plenty large enough for all the bridesmaids to converge for the pre-ceremony photographs. Now that it was getting really close, Sara wasn't nervous but wondered, "Was this all going to come off right?"

She unzipped the garment bag and looked fondly at her wedding dress. Amy said, "If you have any thoughts about backing out, now's the time."

She snapped back, "Not even funny."

Sara's mom said, "Come on girls, there's less than two hours, so let's get going."

Getting into their dresses and gowns didn't take much time but all the adjusting, hair finessing, and final touches, many of which might have to be redone at the last minute, was an ongoing process. The photographer was quick to get any embarrassing shots. By the time all the bridesmaids showed up, they were as ready as they were going to be. The photographer then took over, directing everyone into positions for the best group photos.

With all that done, Sara sneaked a peek out into the church that, although not a cathedral, had several large columns holding up a towering ceiling. The altar was decorated with multicolored drapes, ribbons, flowers, and flickering candles. Despite the cloudy conditions, rays of light streamed in through the stained-glass windows, reflecting their colors off the specks of dust in the air, looking somewhat like the rainbow she was hoping for. Sara was relieved to see the pews filling up, weather aside.

The ushers were dutifully escorting the bride's family to the left, groom's to the right. She spotted Mr. Nichols sitting on the left side, way in the back. He had declined an invite to be one of the groomsmen, saying this was an affair for immediate family and friends. As she looked at him, she flashed back on how much he has meant to her and couldn't think of many better friends than he. She ducked back into the room, knowing it was almost time.

Everyone was gabbing when there was a knock at the door. It was her dad, who told them that Ryan and Randy were in place at the altar and the bridesmaids should line up with the groomsmen in the vestibule. The ring bearer, a nephew of Ryan's, and the flower girl, Sara's cousin, were just outside the door. When her dad saw Sara in her wedding dress, he got a big lump in his throat. He walked over, and as he hugged her, whispered something that had tears dripping down both their cheeks. Her mom ran over with a Kleenex and carefully blotted them up and pulled the veil down over Sara's face. She handed her the bouquet, and then used the same Kleenex to wipe away tears of her own.

Someone gave a signal and the organist started playing "Here Comes the Bride." Sara and her father were last in the long, slow procession down the aisle. Waiting on the altar steps were Amy on one side and Ryan on the other. Amy stepped down, lifted Sara's veil, and took her bouquet. Sara looked up at Ryan, who was absolutely transfixed by how beautiful she looked. When he came down the steps, Sara's father shook his hand and stepped aside.

There was a moment of silence as everyone settled down before the priest, dressed in his regal garments, came out of the sacristy and faced the packed church. He greeted them with, "Welcome family and friends. We are gathered here together to witness the union of Ryan and Sara in the bonds of holy matrimony." With that said, he turned to face the altar and started a short mass. When it was complete, he came to the top of the steps, smiled and nodded to Sara. He had known her since she was a little girl.

He stepped down right in front of the betrothed couple and said, "You may present your vows." After those were read, rings and 'I dos' were exchanged, and the priest ended the ceremony with, "In the name of the Holy Spirit, I now solemnly declare you to be husband and wife." He didn't have to say you may kiss the bride—that was already in process. There was applause, tears, and smiles as they walked back down the aisle, this time together.

Heavier rain prevented the usual celebration when the bride and groom walk out the church doors. They just ran straight to Randy's car. When he pulled away, it started a parade of cars all headed to The Captain's Inn. When they got there, Ryan, Sara, Randy, and Amy lined up just inside the large, round top doors to welcome the guests as they entered.

When it seemed most of them had arrived, Randy prompted everyone into the parlor, managing to keep an open spot in the center of the dance floor for Ryan and Sara. He nodded to the girl singer in front of the band to start singing "I Will Always Love You." Ryan extended his arm and held out his hand, which Sara accepted. He pulled her in close to him, and as they started to dance, they seemed to melt into one person. Sometimes they swayed with the music, and sometimes they barely moved, seemingly unaware there was anyone else in the room.

Ryan in his tuxedo and Sara in a magnificent dress had everyone's cameras clicking. The official photographer circled them, getting every angle. Sara's parents, knowing they should go pair up with them, couldn't bring themselves to break the spell. Finally Sara glanced at her dad as a signal to come onto the dance floor. When Ryan's parents joined in, everyone else was invited onto the floor.

The rest of the afternoon and early evening was all about music, more dancing, toasts, speeches, lots of food, and, of course, cake. Randy's speech had everyone teary eyed again and Amy's, of course, had everyone laughing. The owner of the Inn made an announcement that their Saturday evening dinners here would be free gratis for the next six months. Mr. Nichols told them he had contacted a former associate at the cape and arranged for a personal tour of the space center. With an eight P.M. flight scheduled, Ryan and Sara, after many thank yous and goodbyes, left to drive back to the apartment, where they had stashed everything for the honeymoon trip. Once there they changed, they grabbed their luggage and headed for the airport.

They weren't aware of how long it took to fly to the Daytona Beach International Airport, having spent the entire flight talking about the wedding, the reception, and their future. One of the stewardesses, hearing some of that, asked if it was their wedding day and then announced it on the PA system. That prompted a round of applause. Ryan waved, and Sara blushed.

Night had closed in by the time they landed. They rented a car and headed for the honeymoon suite at one of the swanky hotels right on the beach. The room was more than they had expected—large, exquisitely decorated, and on the top floor. After they unpacked, Sara wandered out onto the balcony and gazed out at the ocean. She wondered, *How could I be so lucky? Perfect husband, perfect wedding, perfect reception, perfect honeymoon suite, and a trip to Cape Canaveral coming up.* For once she didn't even look up at the stars.

Ryan came out and said, "Got everything put away...you're awful quiet out here."

She said, "I was just thinking how great everything went today and what a wonderful setting this is."

He said, "Well maybe I can add to that." He grabbed her and kissed her more passionately than ever before.

She said, "We can't be doing this out here. Let's go inside."

CHAPTER 7
MOON ROCKS

The following morning, Ryan suggested, "Let's get a room service breakfast. Might as well take advantage of all the amenities while we're here."

Following breakfast and cleaning up, they headed for the beach. Some quiet time and mindless fun were warranted after the hectic activities of the last few weeks.

A couple days of shopping, an ocean tour, and intimate dinners gave way to a seventy-five-mile drive to Disney World. Since they hadn't known each other as kids, they planned to make up for that all in one day. Their goal was to go on every ride but long lines and too many people squashed that plan. Still it was a full day that left them stuffed with hot dogs, cinnamon buns, and all the other junk food they couldn't resist. On the drive back to the hotel, they agreed to no dinner and some kind of exercise tomorrow. They started on the exercise that evening, taking advantage of one of the benefits of being married.

Up early the next morning, they had a small breakfast and then went down to the beach for a two-mile run followed by a dip in the ocean. Later they discovered a small shack right on the sand for lunch. It was late afternoon when they got back to their room and started to talk about the trip to the cape.

Mr. Nichols had given them the phone number of his associate, Tom Jeffords, so Ryan called him. As soon as Ryan mentioned Mr. Nichols, Tom spoke up, "Ah, Bob Nichols, we sure miss him around here. I understand you and your wife are future scientists and would like a tour of this place."

Ryan said, "Yes, when it would be convenient."

Mr. Jeffords replied, "It's a good time here now because there's not much going on, so I could give you the grand tour any day this week."

Ryan suggested the day after next and they agreed on a time and place to meet. When he hung up, Sara was jumping up and down all around the room.

They slept in the next morning, had a late breakfast in the downstairs restaurant, and then drove over to Embry-Riddle Aeronautical University. It's the world's largest and a very highly regarded educational institution. They had taken a virtual tour online when they first heard about it but wanted to see the campus up close. Anyway, it was a good way to make this day go by faster.

The drive to the space center would be just under eighty miles. The meeting was scheduled for 10 A.M.; Sara was up at six. When Ryan awoke, he saw most of her outfits spread out on the furniture. She was excited about the tour, nervous about meeting Mr. Jeffords, and couldn't decide what to wear. Ryan, trying to wind her down a bit, said, "Sara it's not how you look but your knowledge and dedication to science that will impress Mr. Jeffords."

She said, "You're right. I'll call down for breakfast and start getting ready."

They were on the road by eight thirty, and most of their conversation in the car centered around NASA's historic milestones. They arrived just before ten, and Mr. Jeffords came to the lobby to greet them. He introduced himself, shook Ryan's hand, and then turned to Sara and said, "You must be Sara."

She confirmed, "I am."

"Bob Nichols has spoken to me about you several times. He tells me you're one of the few people who saw the comet approaching Mars all those years ago." Sara was embarrassed but Ryan was beaming with pride. Mr. Jeffords continued, "Here, we are one of the principal organizations dealing with outer space and only one of our astronomers was watching that night. We may run into him on the tour." He turned back to Ryan and said, "I understand your passion is planetary geology. You two make quite a pair—what she observes with her telescope, you want to actually go pickup and examine. Well let's get started. I'll let you know when we're someplace where you won't be allowed to take pictures."

He first took them around to several of the standard exhibits, including the Astronaut Hall of Fame, Mission Control Center, the Rocket Garden, and a giant Saturn 5 Rocket. At one point, they got to step inside a mockup of the space shuttle. There was no way they could realize it was a precursor to a life-changing event in their future.

One exhibit especially interesting to Sara was the Eyes on the Universe, where there were examples of NASA's 3D Space Telescopes. As she was admiring the display, a gentleman walked up that Mr. Jeffords introduced to Ryan as Jeff Stark. He then turned and said, "And this is Sara Taylor, now Sara Arness."

Mr. Stark excitedly said, "You were the nine-year-old who saw the comet that struck Phobos live!"

"Yep, that was me a long time ago now" Sara said.

"Are you still into astronomy?" Mr. Stark asked.

She answered, "Yes. Ryan and are on our honeymoon, and when we get back, I start my PhD and he starts his in planetary geology."

He asked Sara, "Would you like to see the photos I took that night?"

"That would be awesome," Sara said.

As they walked toward his office, he said, "I understand you two know Bob Nichols."

Ryan explained, "Yes, quite a guy…he has been one of the driving forces behind Sara's passion for science since her early high school days."

"And what drove you toward planetary geology?" asked Mr. Stark.

"I found a meteorite when I was a kid, and the fascination just never went away."

Jeff repeated Ryan's comment, "The fascination never went away," and added, "That's an excellent way to explain the passion of almost every scientist here."

When they got to his office, he pulled a folder out of a filing cabinet and handed it to Sara. There they were…the images that have been in her mind's eye all these years.

"These are it exactly!" she exclaimed.

Jeff said, "Those are prints that you can keep."

Mr. Jeffords interrupted, "Well we have to get moving. I want take Ryan to the Exploring the Moon display."

Jeff ended with, "Nice meeting you both. Maybe you can join us some day."

Ryan's pulse quickened as they got close to the Exploring the Moon display. He had read you could touch an actual moon rock there. The rock was on a pedestal in front of a glass case containing several others. The attendant told him he could touch it but not pick it up.

As Ryan reached out, he couldn't believe he was about to touch something that had been picked up on the Moon by one of our astronauts. He expected a rough surface, but it was quite smooth, having been fondled by thousands of fingers over the years. The attendant asked if he knew what kind of rock it was. Of course Ryan correctly identified it as basalt.

"Very good. Do you know any of the others in the case?"

Ryan said, "The one on the left is anorthosite. There's breccia, and that looks like regolith."

An impressed attendant said, "Very good. You're the first one in a long time to know them all." It was Sara's turn to be proud.

Mr. Jeffords told the attendant, "I kind of set you up. Ryan here is an aspiring planetary geologist."

The attendant said, "Well in that case, you get the special treatment. Have a look," and swung a microscope over the rock.

Ryan focused in on it, and after trying all the different lenses, asked, "Can you take a photo of this?"

The attendant said, "I can." Within seconds there was the sound of a printer running behind the display.

As Ryan continued to stare into the eyepieces, Sara said to Mr. Jeffords, "We'll never get him away from here."

Ryan eventually pried himself away to look at the photo, and Sara took the opportunity to ask, "What's next?"

Next was a trip to the center's cafeteria for lunch. When they sat down to eat, Jeff Stark came in and asked if he could join them. Soon he and Sara had the photos he gave her spread out on the table. They spent several minutes comparing notes about their common experiences with the comet and the missing ex-moon. He asked if she still kept up with the latest news about Phobos.

Sara answered immediately saying, "Yes, and even though it has disappeared from the view from even the most powerful telescopes, it's never far from my thoughts."

Jeff suggested, "Since you probably know as much as anyone about the Phobos incident, you should write a book."

Sara said, "It's something that's been on my mind for years, so I may get to it someday when I have the time."

He went on to ask her several probing questions, including what kind of telescope she had, what books she had read, what her major had been, etc. Meanwhile, Mr. Jeffords was talking to Ryan about geology and physics and asking him similar questions. They both got the feeling they were being interviewed.

After lunch they resumed the tour, visiting several of those 'off limit, no pictures allowed' places and meeting some of the top engineers. The entire tour ended up taking almost five hours. When Mr. Jeffords escorted them back to the lobby, he handed them his business card saying, "You are both very highly regarded by Bob Nichols, who pulls a lot of weight around here. I hope you'll consider interviewing with us when you're finished with college. Have a safe trip back."

On the way back, there would be short periods of silence followed by one of them asking do you remember seeing this or talking to that engineer? Ryan still couldn't believe he had touched an actual Moon rock, and Sara kept looking at the photos from Mr. Stark. The drive back seemed much quicker than the drive there.

That evening they had dinner at the restaurant on the first floor of the hotel. Ryan delighted in being able to just write their room number on the check. When heading back to the elevator, they wandered into the lounge where a small band was playing quiet mood music. There were some couples dancing and Ryan asked, "Wanna dance?"

Sara said, "You mean like at a wedding?"

He said, "Come on, smarty."

After a couple of dances they sat down at a table and Ryan said, "I'm going to have a beer. What would you like?"

Sara, just twenty-one, said, "I'll try one."

When it arrived, she took one sip and got that scrunched up look on her face. Ryan said, "I'll get you a Coke."

A young couple who had also been dancing was sitting at the next table. The gentleman leaned over and inquired, "Excuse me, didn't we see you two taking the tour at Kennedy Space Center today?"

Sara spoke up, "Why yes, we were there. What did you think of it?"

He said, "We really liked it. We're here on vacation and thought you might be too."

Introductions followed, along with a pleasant evening of exchanging stories. Sara and Ryan played down their interest in science, not wanting to dominate the conversation. They met for lunch the following day, but their new friends had a flight out later that afternoon. Ryan and Sara would be on a plane the day after next themselves.

It was dark when a bumpy landing at the airport near the university jarred them both awake. As soon as the plane door opened, they took the long walk down the jet way and made their way to the baggage claim area. They were surprised to see Amy and Randy waiting there to greet them.

Randy filled them in on how the reception had gone on for a couple more hours after they left. Ryan and Sara raved about the great time they had on their honeymoon, and when Randy asked to hear all about the tour of the space center, Amy thought, *Oh no, more nerd talk*.

When the rehash of the tour was over, Amy told them she had cleaned up the apartment and moved all her stuff back to her mom's, where she would be staying for the summer. Then the buzzer sounded, and their suitcases slid down the ramp and onto the turnstile. Ryan grabbed them, they said goodbye and headed for the parking lot.

It was a short drive to the apartment, and when Sara unlocked the door, she got a strange feeling. After living there for four years with Amy, this was now going to be her and Ryan's first place. She pushed open the door and was put at ease, thanks to Amy, seeing a big banner on the wall that read 'HOME SWEET HOME.' Further inside, they found wedding presents piled all over the living room. They dropped off their luggage and went for a burger.

The following morning, they drove out to Ryan's parents' house so he could get his things. When they arrived, Ryan started packing up the car while Sara visited with his mother in the kitchen. His mom wanted to hear all about the honeymoon, something Sara was eager to relate.

When Ryan's things were stowed away back at the apartment, they both flopped down on the couch, and he let out a big exhale.

She asked, "What was that for?"

He replied, "There were so many details leading up to this very moment, but we did it. We did everything, and now here it is, the start of our life together."

She leaned over, kissed him, and said, "Isn't it wonderful?"

CHAPTER 8
RACHEL

With the wedding over, the plan was to divide their time between their current jobs and working on PhD degrees. They had both qualified for accelerated programs based on their grade point averages and strong backgrounds in their specific area of research. Still, it was estimated to take up to three years to complete them. It was a demanding agenda that could be tough on a newly married couple. There would be weeks when they saw little of each other because of schedules that didn't mesh, but their love for each other and their chosen careers would always smooth out any rough spots.

One Friday morning, toward the end of his PhD program, Ryan was told to report to the dean's office. On the way there he thought, *My grades are good, and I haven't missed too many classes the last couple of years. What could it be?*

Once in his office, the dean invited him to sit down and asked, "Are you missing a class to be here?"

Ryan responded, "No, sir."

The dean began, "We have been following your studies here at the university and frankly are impressed by your pragmatic approach to geology and your proficiency in physics." Ryan was quick to thank him but still somewhat bemused. The dean continued, "We would like to sign you up for a research position with the geology department when you finish your PhD. You would have a choice of projects, and I think you would be satisfied with the salary. Of course there would be no charge for the remainder of your classes."

Ryan was stunned. None of his professors had hinted at anything like this. Many possibilities and doubts immediately flashed through his head. Working in a lab might mean he would have to forgo the search and discover part of geology he loved so much. It would also mean a commitment to live in this city long term. Knowing he couldn't possibly make any such decision without talking to Sara, he apologetically told the dean he would talk this over with his wife and get back to him.

After the day's classes, he hurried home to get Sara's input but forgot she had the afternoon shift at the restaurant. He paced around the apartment, having alternating thoughts for and against accepting the dean's offer. Up until now, he had been contented just learning about the subject he loved but here he was being asked to commit to a career.

It was almost two hours before Sara came in the door. Ryan walked right up, hugged her, and said, "Have I got news for you!"

She countered, "I have news for you, too."

Ryan relented, "Okay, what's yours?"

"Let me get my coat off and let's go sit down," she said.

Ryan thought, *Oh no, sit down news.*

When they got settled on the couch, she took a breath and started, "I haven't been regular for a couple of months, which isn't unusual for me, but I bought one of those home test kits anyway."

Ryan spoke up, "Something you've been keeping secret, huh?"

Sara snickered and said, "Oh, Ryan dearest, we both know all of each other's secrets by now. No, this was just a suspicion that had little chance of being confirmed. But get ready for a shock...when I took the test today, it showed positive. I'll have to go to my doctor to find out for sure."

An astounded Ryan got an instant glow on his face. He asked if she had an appointment with the doctor yet.

She said, "It's next Monday morning." Adding, "It's not one hundred percent, but these test kits are pretty reliable."

He stuttered, "If-if it is, do you keep working? D-do you keep going to school? Is there anything that I can do? I don't know how any of this works."

She answered, "I would probably have to stop work at some point, but nothing else would change until after the birth."

By now Ryan had almost completely forgotten what he wanted to tell her until she asked, "Now, what's your news?"

Taking a second to even recall what it was, he said, "Well it doesn't seem nearly as important anymore, but I've been offered a position with the geology department at the university when I finish my PhD."

"What would you be doing?" she asked.

He answered, "It would be research, but I didn't get all the details yet. I told the dean you and I would talk it over, and I would get back to him."

She offered, "Well it would certainly dictate where we would live."

Ryan said, "One of the first things I thought about, too. One good thing though, the rest of my classes would be free."

Sara pondered, "Hmm, if I am pregnant, it looks to me like a godsend. It would certainly give us some stability going forward, and we could do some long-term planning. But is this something you want?"

He replied, "Yes, I would love doing research if I could I still be out in the field sometimes. So when I go see the dean on Monday, you're alright if I accept?"

She reassured him, "As long as you're happy, so am I."

Ryan, still somewhat dazed about the possible pregnancy, asked, "So will your doctor be able to tell right away?"

"There are some signs she can look for, but a blood test is the for-sure test. If they have a lab in their office, I will know right away," she explained.

It was a weekend of apprehension, anxiety, excitement, and a lot of discussion about what it would be like to be parents. When Monday finally arrived, Ryan was off to the university and Sara to the doctor.

The dean supplied Ryan with satisfactory answers to all his questions, and when he learned how much the salary was, he accepted the research position. He only had six months left of his PhD program, after which he would quit his job at Barnes and Noble and be able to spend much more time with Sara and then, possibly a baby.

He had to work that afternoon but was dying to find out if Sara had gotten the results of the potentially life-changing test. Midafternoon, while he was cataloging a shipment of books, he looked up to see Sara approaching. She had an expressionless look on her face and just asked, "Did you accept the research position?"

He said, "Yeah, I did."

Before he could ask anything else, she followed with, "Good, we'll be able use the health insurance." He immediately knew what that meant and asked how far along she was. "Just two months," was her reply.

Not something they had planned on, but both were elated. Sara was proud to tell her parents and Ryan his.

Not much changed over the next few months except Sara's waist, which had all but disappeared. She'd turned Amy's old bedroom into a nursery with some new and some hand-me-down furniture. No color scheme was applied because they had decided not to learn the sex before the birth. Ryan was almost done with classes and looking forward to his first 'real' job, and Sara had plans to work right up until the birth. That plan changed one night in the middle of her seventh month.

Ryan had long since fallen into a deep, dark state of REM sleep when he sensed he might be shivering from something cold. He rolled over on his back and got his eyelids about half open, only to see Sara's face just six inches away. She was violently shaking him and saying, "Ryan, wake up. Wake up, Ryan!"

Eyes wide open now, he asked, "What's wrong?"

She told him she had been woken up by some pain in her lower abdomen and discovered some bleeding. He asked if she was concerned enough for a trip to the emergency room. She said, "I think so, yes."

He immediately jumped up, and when Sara got out of the bed he could see the blood on the front of her pajamas. He quickly dressed as Sara put on a long coat and grabbed a pair of jeans and a blouse. The hospital was a few miles away, but at that time of night, there was little traffic, and any red lights or stop signs were carefully ignored by Ryan.

He left the car in front of the emergency door and helped Sara inside. The nurse at the check-in desk asked what the problem was, and Sara told her she was pregnant and just opened the long coat she was wearing. When the nurse saw the blood, she immediately picked up the phone and called for an orderly. Within seconds, Sara was being wheeled to an examination room and Ryan diverted into a small waiting room.

He temporarily ducked out to park his car, and then it was one long hour before a nurse came out and motioned for him to come in. Sara, up and dressed in jeans and blouse, was looking much less upset. The doctor told him they didn't find anything to be immediately concerned about, but she should take it easy and see her gynecologist as soon as possible.

On the drive home, a still anxious Ryan suggested, "I think you should give notice at the restaurant right away." Then he asked, "Are you worried or scared?"

She thought for a minute and said, "Ask me that again after my doctor's appointment." Which took place a few days later.

After a complete physical exam and an ultrasound, the doctor told her the bleeding and pain were most likely caused by a condition known as preterm labor. She went on to say, "If it was earlier in your term, I would be concerned about a premature birth, but you're so far along, and if it doesn't happen again, everything should be just fine. Call if you get the slightest hint of a re-occurrence, and we'll see you right away. Also, let's schedule biweekly appointments from now on."

Two weeks later, Sara was a stay-at-home future mom. She continued her PhD classes online and started to seriously think about writing that book she had been contemplating. She would call it *Phobos the Lost Moon*. Secretly she still held out hope for Mr. Nichols's theory that, by some trick of physics, it would return someday.

Right on schedule, Ryan completed his PhD and started in the geology department. He let his boss know his wife was about to give birth and he may have to take some time off. His boss said, "No problem. The university has a two-week paid leave for a birth in the family."

When Sara was in her final month, she had had enough of being pregnant with parents, relatives, and friends calling to ask how are you, is everything alright, when is your due date, do you know if it's a boy or girl? In her ninth month, there was another middle of the night event when Ryan, dead to the world, was shaken awake again and Sara saying, "Ryan, wake up! Wake up, Ryan."

Eyes wide open this time, he asked, "Problems again?"

She said, "No I'm having contractions that are very close together this time."

That prompted another speedy trip to the hospital without the interference of red lights or stop signs. They hadn't taken any Lamaze classes, but Ryan planned to stay with her the entire time.

It was thirteen hours before a healthy, six pounds, nine ounces Rachel made her grand entrance. She wasn't crying, just squirming around as if she wasn't comfortable in her new environment. When the nurse cleaned her up and placed her in Sara's arms, any thoughts of contractions, months of worry after the bleeding event, and all the unpleasantries of pregnancy didn't just fade away, they all but disappeared.

Sara had read several books about newborn care, so felt well prepared. The two nights in the hospital didn't dispel that, but the nurses were there to calm her down when Rachel would do something that might have sent her into a panic. Once back home, Rachel would bunk in a bassinet right next to their bed.

Turns out, 'sleeping like a baby' doesn't necessarily mean peace and quiet. They weren't quite prepared for the scary noises newborns often make. There are grunts, snores, choking sounds, disruptions in their breathing, and others that can't even be described. Sleeping for Sara and Ryan was a one-eye-open experience, and any one of these noises meant instantly up, lights on, and wondering if they should rush her to the emergency room. Grandmothers would prove to be the cure for all this insecurity.

CHAPTER 9
THE OBSERVATORY

Eventually Ryan settled into his job at the university, and Sara learned to balance motherhood, online PhD classes, and working on her book. When not at work, Ryan would pick up many of the chores, giving Sara a break. They were learning to be parents.

It was almost two years before Sara completed her program and started to think about getting a job. Her thoughts drifted back to the incident that had inspired her to get into astronomy in the first place.

As far back as she could remember, she had delighted in looking out her bedroom window at a mountain off in the distance. It was spectacularly tall, and when its peak was covered with snow, she imagined it to be frosting on a cake.

One afternoon, her father drove the family up that mountain and parked at the scenic overlook. The valley below was a magnificent sight of trees, a river that ran through the center of town, and the downtown skyline. Sara strained to see their house, but it was too far away. Her gaze strayed around to the very top of the mountain, where she noticed a strange building with a round roof.

When she asked, her father told her it was the Morris Observatory and inside was a large telescope they used to look up into the sky at the stars and planets. That sounded exciting, but he told her only scientists were allowed to go there. Seeing how disappointed she was, he told her there was a place in town that also has a round roof where there are lights on the ceiling that look like the stars in the sky. He promised to take her there soon.

True to his word, it wasn't long before six-year-old Sara was sitting with her parents in the downtown planetarium, absolutely transfixed by the expanse of simulated stars and celestial bodies projected onto the ceiling. She actually tingled at the thought that someday she might be one of those scientists. And now here she is, hoping to find a way to somehow realize that very goal.

She composed a resume that highlighted her education, her more than fifteen years' experience behind a telescope, and her ability in physics, thanks to Ryan's tutoring. She sent it to the Morris Observatory, not knowing if they were even looking for astronomers. Ryan suggested she should also send it to companies that were advertising for candidates with her qualifications. She did, knowing he was right, but her hope lay with the observatory.

When two weeks went by without any responses, she began to wonder if her resume didn't impress anyone. Ryan told her to be patient, that these things can take time. He was right, as replies dribbled in over the next week. Some weren't going to work because they required relocation. Others requested she travel for a personal interview, and one sent a questionnaire requesting more in-depth information. Unfortunately, the jobs being offered were either for teaching positions or as a research assistant. There was nothing from the observatory. She tried to put her disappointment aside by answering all the suitable responses to her resume.

Then one morning she got a phone call from a woman who introduced herself as Dr. Maya Herschel, Chief Astronomer at the Morris Observatory. She apologized for the delay in responding to her resume and added they didn't have an opening at this time. Sara's heart sank...there went all her hopes and dreams. But instead of saying goodbye, the woman continued, "I showed your resume to some of our engineers, and frankly, we all question that someone your age could have accumulated the degree of knowledge and experience you claim to have. Is there someone I could contact as a reference?"

With a rush of renewed optimism, Sara gave her the name and number for Mr. Nichols. The woman inquired, "Would that be Bob Nichols, the astrophysicist?"

Sara proudly told her, "Yes, I've known him for several years."

Dr. Herschel ended, "I may get back to you after I've talked with him. Goodbye."

Sara picked up Rachel and spun around the room. The surprised two-year-old cried out, "Mommy, no!" Ryan got to hear this story numerous times that evening.

It was several agonizing days before Dr. Herschel called back. She told Sara, "Bob Nichols had no trouble convincing me that you are indeed what you claim to be. I asked him why we hadn't heard about you before this. He explained that all the astronomical work and learning you've done up till now has been mostly in private, so you haven't gotten any notice from the scientific community. He then added that should be rectified when your book gets published. What book? I asked him.

"He replied, 'She had me write the forward to her book she wrote titled *Phobos the Lost Moon.*'" Dr. Herschel said to Sara, "After the call, I thought about taking you on as an intern, but you're far beyond that stage. A more permanent position that might work would involve lots of telescope time, followed by writing technical papers on your observations. Those papers would then be distributed to the astronomical community.

"There was no mention on your resume that you've ever done any technical writing, although Bob did mention your book. Has that been published?"

An overwhelmed Sara blurted out, "No, but I could send you a paper copy."

"Why don't you bring it up here so we can meet...when would be a good time for you?"

For an instant, Sara was speechless. She had just been invited to drive up the very road her father had taken all those years ago, but her destination would be that strange building with the round roof where only scientists were allowed. When they agreed on the following afternoon at two o'clock, Sara had no idea how she was ever going to sleep that night.

Her pulse seemed to go up a tick for every mile on the way to the observatory. After parking, she got out of her car, looked up at the dome, and couldn't help but think this is the place she'd been fantasizing about for most of her life.

Dr. Herschel met her at the door and led her to the observation room. Sara had been in rooms like this before but this one had the largest telescope she had ever seen. As tall as that mountain was, Sara was higher up on cloud nine at that moment. The tour ended in a conference room occupied by several skeptical astronomers and engineers.

What followed was a rigorous question and answer session that could have been intimidating but Sara felt quite at ease. She knew the subject and was able to address all their questions and remarks with conviction. On the way out, Dr. Herschel told her they would all discuss the results of the interview. Then she added, "I know we're all quite anxious to read a book written by someone who actually saw the Phobos incident live. I'll be in touch with you soon."

While driving home, Sara experienced an avalanche of emotions. Had she answered all the questions to their satisfaction? Had she done enough to make them want to hire her? Is this the right place for her first real job? Maybe she should start working on the other responses she received. Somehow she would try to put it all out of her mind for now.

When the phone rang the following afternoon, Sara ran to answer it, hoping to hear Dr. Herschel's voice. It was Amy asking if it was a good time for a visit. In a way, Sara was relieved and always happy to hear from her BFF. By now, Amy had completed her EdD and secured a job as an administrative assistant to the dean of a local college.

Since graduation, she and Amy would get together or talk on the phone as much as possible. Amy would often baby-sit, and she and Rachel had become great friends. In fact, when she arrived, Rachel ran to her wanting to be picked up. Sara was anxious to tell her how the job search was going, but she could tell Amy was just bubbling over to tell her something.

Sara asked, "Okay, what's up?"

Amy put Rachel down and started, "Well you know I have been seeing Damon for some time."

Sara sarcastically interjected, "Uh...let's see, that would be the science teacher, right?"

Amy shot back, "Okay, I know it's kind of ironic, but last night he asked me to marry him, and I said yes!"

That started a celebration akin to when Sara announced her engagement to Ryan. Rachel laughed and danced around with them, having no idea why. Sara demanded, "I need to know all about it." Amy excitedly gushed out all the intimate details and, of course, asked Sara to be her maid of honor and Rachel to be the flower girl.

It wasn't until the following week Dr. Herschel called to tell her everyone had been quite impressed with her book and with her performance in the conference room. She went over the salary, benefits, hours, vacation package, etc. and asked if she would be interested. Sara tried to stay calm as she accepted but internally she was doing cartwheels. They picked a day and time for Sara to drive back up, complete the paperwork, and get started. A six-year-old's dream that she might become 'one of those scientists' was actually coming true.

CHAPTER 10

LIFE MOVES ON

Sara was absolutely enchanted with her new job, but it created a need for a daytime sitter for Rachel. Both grandmothers eagerly volunteered, and an agreeable schedule was eventually worked out. Amy and Damon's wedding came off as planned, and flower girl Rachel all but stole the show.

With their now substantial income, Sara's book got published and soon became a best seller among the astronomical set. After a while, the technical papers she was producing at the observatory became a must read for anyone researching cosmic bodies. Ryan's desire to continue with some field work was realized when he was tagged by the university to cover any meteor strikes or any other geological anomalies occurring in the world. Eventually he started work on a book of his own titled *The Geology of Our Solar System*. Their years of study and dedication were beginning to pay off as they were achieving goals that were set when, as youngsters, simple events had aroused their scientific curiosity.

Just after Rachel's fourth birthday, Ryan brought up the point that soon they would have to be thinking about a school for her, so maybe they should consider looking for a house in a good school zone. Possibly even one that's closer to the observatory to cut down on Sara's drive.

Sara responded, "That sounds good. Maybe next week we can look for a realtor."

Both sets of parents were a gold mine of information for that venture, having been through the real estate grind several times.

It didn't take long for them to find the right house, and during the move, Rachel spotted her mom's old lava lamp and asked what it was. When Sara plugged it in, Rachel's eyes lit up brighter than the lamp. Sara said, "We'll put it in your new bedroom."

As darkness was falling, Ryan went into Rachel's bedroom to comfort her with a bedtime story. Sara, not wanting to deal with all the boxes and items still scattered around, stepped out the back door onto the porch. She could just make out the outline of the mountain off in the distance, but the observatory was way too small to pick out. She looked around the yard and spotted the perfect place for Nexter.

Darkness and fatigue from the move eventually drove her back into the house. She watched Ryan quietly close the door to Rachel's bedroom and asked, "Did she get to sleep alright?"

Ryan said, "She did. I read her a story, but I think the glow from the lava lamp soothed any uneasiness she had about her new bedroom. She made me leave it on."

A reminiscent Sara smiled and said, "Worked for me."

After the house was all settled, Ryan found time to finish his book, which, when published, was well received by the geological society. That, along with his research at the university and work in the field, gained him some well-deserved notoriety. So much so that he was invited to speak at several geological conventions and was eventually appointed head of the lab department.

The next few years saw Sara and Ryan settle into a comfortable routine of work and family life, with Rachel being thrilled to start school.

CHAPTER 11
THE RETURN

By now, over twenty years have passed since Phobos, almost completely forgotten, had been driven from its one-time charge of orbiting Mars. Most astronomers, including Sara, were busily tracking the return of Halley's Comet on its seventy-six-year periodic cycle through our solar system.

They were intrigued to learn that ground based telescopes had detected a large asteroid-like object, far out in space, possibly traveling in our direction. Months of observation determined it was a distant 480 million miles out, traveling at a speed of about 11,500 miles per hour. Being much farther out than most detected bodies raised suspicion that this one must be unusually large. If it eventually proved to be coming our way, a possibility many astronomers were rightly concerned about, it would happen in just over two and a half years.

Could it be Phobos? Most scientists thought not, arguing that many of the theories about its route through the Milky Way had been debunked years ago. There is an intriguing passage in Sara's book that addressed the issue as well as any others that reads:

> *The tracking of Phobos's travels after its rude displacement all those years ago raises suspicion that, given the direction it traveled away from Mars and the future location of Saturn on its twenty-nine-year journey around the Sun, those two bodies seem slated to cross paths. Far enough apart and Phobos would just streak on past; too*

close and it would fall prey to the lure of Saturn's gravity and go into a free fall, gaining velocity all the way down to a mortal crash on the surface. Somewhere in between and it could get caught in Saturn's satellite capture zone and stay locked to it forever.

There is also the remote possibility that it might just come under Saturn's gravitational influence and experience a phenomenon known as the slingshot effect. A chance event that would have it swing around the planet's perimeter, gain acceleration, and get hurled back out into space. Then, no longer on a trek to escape the solar system, it would continue its nomadic wandering in a new slingshot imposed direction. Perhaps even to retrace its journey initiated by the comet impact as seen by this young stargazer.

Yet any notions about this particular object were just speculation since it was still at too great a distance to reveal its actual size and shape for any kind of positive identification.

Continued tracking yielded a more accurate projection of its flight path, which began to show that, whatever it was, would pass through Earth's orbit at a relatively safe distance. This news, of worldwide interest, was at the same time both a relief and an intriguing opportunity to get a closer look at this cosmic traveler.

Time and the world's most powerful telescopes eventually brought the sighting into sharper focus, and its unique shape revealed, much to the surprise of many, that it was, in fact, the return of Phobos. Speculation was that its return was potentially brought about by the slingshot effect, which would be the 'trick of physics' once suggested by Mr. Nichols. Not yet done having run-ins with other celestial bodies, this latest data also showed it to be a mathematical certainty that it was going to have a close encounter with Halley's Comet, which was on its way back out of our neighborhood.

It seemed to be on a mission to prove the adage that our solar system functions much like a vast game of three-dimensional billiards just after the break shot. However, unlike on a pool table, this is conducted on a grand scale, with cosmic bodies randomly interacting with each other at the mercy of the laws of physics. With that reality in mind, it was not entirely surprising that Phobos and Halley's Comet managed to pass close enough to gravitationally disrupt each other's courses.

Once again Phobos had been shepherded by another celestial object. Its new course had major observatories coming forth with frightening predictions of a better than ninety percent chance of an impact with Earth. If they proved to be correct, it would occur, as originally predicted, in less than three years. This realization was especially alarming to the scientific community because an object the size of Phobos wasn't simply just another asteroid, it was a potential threat to all life on Earth.

CHAPTER 12
ROCKETS

Sixty-five million years ago, an asteroid is known to have struck the Earth on what is now the northern coast of Yucatan. The global devastation caused by that impact brought an end to the two-hundred-million yearlong Age of the Dinosaurs. With Phobos being two to three times more massive than that earlier asteroid, it seemed almost prophetic to realize the name Phobos, in Greek, translates to FEAR.

To head off a repeat of such an event, it was universally agreed some form of immediate defensive action needed to be taken. An emergency meeting was convened by The International Science Council based in Paris. Their main objective was to determine the best method to deal with this NEO (Near Earth Object). Objects like Phobos have been under observation and analysis for decades by most of the major nations. Countless teams of scientists are dedicated to finding methods of eliminating or deflecting such things. Yet no plausible approach to the problem had ever gained universal acceptance. But now, with all humanity facing a dinosaur-like extinction, the council must somehow choose one from a list of unproven options.

One being considered was a radiation burst. The execution of which involves firing a rocket with a nuclear warhead at the threat, shattering it into small pieces. Hopefully most would scatter off in harmless, non-Earth threatening directions. Any that continued on a path toward Earth would, optimistically, be small enough to burn up in our atmosphere.

Another possible choice, kinetic impaction, would be carried out by sending one or more large, high-speed rockets crashing into the body of an approaching near-Earth object. This could deflect the object into a different trajectory, steering it away from Earth's orbital path.

Deflection Thrusting would put a small lander on the would-be threat that would use a solar powered propulsion engine to exert a small amount of force over a long period of time, ultimately altering its course just enough to mitigate the threat.

In due course, all but kinetic impacts were rejected as either being impossible to achieve in the limited time available, impractical, or too unpredictable in terms of effect. Kinetic impact, scientific jargon for bumping into it, is described by Isaac Newton's first law of motion as "a force that affects a moving object." In this case, the force would be supplied by the impact of a rocket, and Phobos would be the moving object.

Bolstering the reasoning behind this selection was the curious discovery that since its close encounter with Haley's Comet, Phobos had begun to emit a faint flash of light every seven seconds, much like a lighthouse beacon. This immediately triggered a flurry of speculation as to the true nature of what they were seeing. Could it be some alien communication signal?

One of the planetary geologists on the council came up with a bizarre hypothesis about this mystery. He proposed the comet that knocked Phobos out of orbit had struck right in the center of Stickney Crater. The tremendous amount of heat generated by such an impact would have melted most of the comet's ice, causing the resultant water to fill up the crater. The water would have been contained inside the crater by the cap of ice still exposed to the extreme cold of outer space. Then that cold temperature, almost -500 degrees, would have almost immediately refrozen all the water, leaving the crater filled with solid ice.

Furthermore Phobos's encounter with Haley's Comet may have pulled it into an alignment where the surface of this ice could be, once every seven seconds, facing directly at the many telescopes observing it. Consequently, the flashes could be just a reflection of our own sunlight. The seven second interval between flashes would indicate it must be rotating around its long axis, and that axis would be perfectly aligned with its flight path toward Earth.

This strange behavior would give it the ballistics of an enormous bullet coming straight at us. The rotation would also give it some of the properties of a gyroscope keeping it on a rigid course despite the effect of outside forces.

Accepting all this as accurate led to the realization that it could take several rocket impacts to have any influence on its deadly aim.

The council elected to, as quickly as possible, make ready up to five large impact rockets. Designing and building these rockets would be a joint venture by all the technically advanced countries around the world. Such cooperation would be sorely needed to complete such state-of-the-art machines in the limited time available. Even so, it was estimated to take up to twenty of the remaining months.

They would blast off in sequence from their respective countries, following each other at two hundred fifty mile increments, a distance considered miniscule in the boundless realm of outer space. The force and accuracy required to have the desired effect would make it extremely difficult, if not impossible, for all the rockets to make a direct hit. To up the odds of success, each rocket would share the guidance calculations made during its attempted impact run with the remaining rockets. This would be accomplished using FSO (Free-Space Optical) communication, a fast laser wireless system used in the vacuum of space. Computers in the remaining rockets would then use this information to make increasingly more precise calculations for their attempt at a direct hit.

At blast off time for these rockets, Phobos would be an alarming eighty-seven million miles, or just under eleven months, from Earth. Maximum speed would have them meeting up with the menace in three months. If they weren't successful at coaxing it off its collision course, humanity's time on Earth could be down to less than a year.

The first rocket, built to test some aspects of the design, was launched and sent into the ocean, a necessary precaution. The second one, testing accuracy and speed, was sent crashing into the Earth's moon, something roundly disputed at the United Nations. By the time several more were completed, further testing was precluded because dealing with the disaster speeding toward our precious planet could no longer wait.

Around the world, the five large, impressive impact rockets were sitting on launch pads, prepared to blast off. The synchronous countdown had been in process for days, and everything had been checked and rechecked. When the countdown got to zero, the engines of the first of the five rockets came to life. It slowly lifted off from its launch pad at the Uchinoura Space Center in

Japan, picked up speed, and disappeared into the stratosphere. Four others followed in a perfectly timed progression.

All space-based telescopes, normally dedicated to outer space investigation, were re-positioned to monitor their progress. Forward looking telescopic cameras, located in the tip of each rocket would, when in range, beam back close up images of Phobos during its attempted assault. All of humanity prayed that this 'caravan of hope' would be their salvation.

CHAPTER 13
THE IMPACTS

The five rockets, spaced precisely at their two hundred fifty mile separations, were programmed to strike Phobos on its long axis and as close to its center as possible. This was a mathematically calculated sweet spot that would have maximum effect. The closing speed between the rockets and Phobos would be over seven miles per second, but the computer's tracking calculations wouldn't be started until each rocket was within two hundred fifty miles of Phobos. This left just over thirty seconds between each rocket's, hoped for, kinetic impact.

The calculations couldn't be started sooner because the rocket's cameras, even though state-of-the-art, weren't capable of delivering detailed enough video for the computer's algorithms. Waiting for this train of rockets to catch up to Phobos was a frustrating time for all of humanity. During the entire chase, the forward-facing cameras only transmitted an image of the star speckled blackness of space.

Right on schedule they came within range, and the first rocket, designated Rocket1, started streaming detailed images back to a very relieved Earth. It locked onto the target and started to calculate and re-calculate its own angle and speed, firing small rocket bursts to get lined up. All of its guidance correction data was being transmitted back to the other rockets via the FSO wireless network. Even at the speed of light, it took up to four minutes for the images to reach the Earth. When shown on worldwide television, people were getting their first close up look at Phobos but didn't realize they weren't seeing their hoped-for salvation in real time.

Before the two closed in on each other, Phobos only appeared as a small dot traveling from right to left on the screen. The rocket's computer labored at full processing power attempting to compute Phobos's exact speed, something that wouldn't be known for sure until the two were in very close proximity to each other.

At their closing speed, it was only seconds before Phobos, moving toward the center of the screen, seemed to get larger and larger, as if under a zoom lens. As the detail in the video got sharper and sharper, the computer selected a spot on Phobos without any craters or pockmarks as the target area for all the rockets. Rocket1 continued making small course corrections while conducting a life and death exercise in Euclidean geometry and Newtonian physics, all being orchestrated in nanoseconds by an inanimate computer program.

As the two adversaries got closer and closer, Phobos quickly grew larger and, for an instant, filled the screen, looking like a preview of it falling to Earth. But then, just as quickly, it shot off the left side of the screen. The rocket, not having gotten Phobos's precise speed worked out in time, passed several miles behind it. Its camera was left displaying the cold, dark universe it was now doomed to roam forever.

The next rocket in line, Rocket2, started its approach and with the guidance data from Rocket1, had a head start on calculating Phobos's speed. Its camera was now transmitting the video back to Earth, and to the viewers, it seemed as if they were watching an instant replay. Again, as the two got close, Phobos seemed to zoom up in size and began to fill the screen. Anticipation soared as it was perfectly lined up to strike in the center of the long axis. Then, milliseconds before impact, hope was dashed again as the rocket, way too far north of center, skipped across the top surface of the elusive rock and joined Rocket1 on an endless tour of the cosmos.

Rocket3 was up next and with all the accumulated guidance data, should be primed to score a direct hit. Another instant replay played out on the screens of a now dismayed and doubtful worldwide audience. The rocket quickly lined up dead center, making it obvious the guidance computers had the math all worked out. This time, Phobos zoomed up to a point where they could make out small rocks and even pebbles on the surface just before their screens went blank. Guarded optimism arose as this was taken as a sure sign of an impact. Maybe, just maybe, it would produce some or all of the deflection needed to misdirect this terror.

Rocket4 approached, and as Phobos began to zoom up again, it rotated around to a point where, for a fleeting instant, the screen was filled with the spot where Rocket3 had just struck. Disappointingly, there was no big impact mark. Rockets this large and powerful should have left a crater with rocket debris scattered about but there was only a slightly disturbed spot with a dark area in the center. Had it just bounced or ricocheted off the surface? Rocket4 made its attack, and when the screen went blank, there was no big cheer...just somber confusion.

As Rocket5 zeroed in, its images showed the same disappointing kind of impact marks left by Rocket3 and Rocket4. These two previous hits were less than sixty yards apart, so accuracy was not a problem. When Rocket5's camera went blank, everyone was left wondering, what had they just witnessed? Success or failure? The answer to that would only come with more tracking over the next few days and weeks. In the meantime, an uneasy population clambered for an explanation for the visually unsatisfying results.

Among the many conflicting theories as to why there wasn't a more pronounced impact area, one began to resonate with the scientific community. It was Ryan who put forth a paper wherein he stated that, unlike the common belief that Phobos was a solid chunk of rock, he had long subscribed to the alternate theory it was a porous body about twenty-five to thirty percent hollow. Upon studying the video, he believed the rockets had just passed through the soft iron and rocky outer layer and disappeared into the central void. No surface impact and no deflection, unfortunately, led to the conclusion that Phobos was, in all likelihood, continuing on its deadly course.

More intense tracking showed there may have been a very slight deflection, but its gyroscopic effect could eventually negate it. Still on point to come under the influence of our gravitational field, its angle of approach guaranteed there would be no saving sling shot effect. While plummeting down through our atmosphere, it would constantly pick up speed, reaching terminal velocity before crashing to the ground. Now there seemed to be no way to stop the sure death that was streaking through space, like all other astronomical bodies, following the universal laws of physics.

CHAPTER 14
GRAVITY

With the possible termination of all life on Earth, political, territorial, religious, and financial conflicts had little meaning. Churches became popular places as people had a sudden renewed interest in religion. Unfortunately some places degraded into chaos and crime, placing law enforcement in the precarious position of having to decide between quelling the lawlessness or worrying about their own salvation.

The world's population was painfully aware of the exact countdown to the impending disaster. As months turned into weeks, Phobos, a riveting but depressing sight, could be seen with even small amateur telescopes. Before long, it was close enough to discern its potato-like oval shape, making it recognizable as the Martian moon it once was.

Of course Sara was watching all this unfold from the observatory, and to her it seemed unbelievable the event she had once been so excited about was turning into such a disaster. One evening of the final week, she, Ryan, Rachel, Amy and Damon had all gathered in her parents' living room. She and Amy were talking about their high school days. Sara was picking on Amy about the way she would do her hair after a soccer game.

When the reality of the situation returned, Sara sighed, "There is no way such an inspirational piece of my childhood could turn into something so evil. I refuse to believe it. It's just not true. You'll see. Something will happen, and we'll all be fine."

Amy looked at Sara with sadness in her eyes, remembering the last time she saw her friend that determined. "Sara, maybe you were right about us becoming friends and God knows what else, but I'm just not sure this time."

As the end approached, people came together, consoling each other and sharing final words as despair was inevitably setting in. Mothers couldn't let their children go, fathers cursed the very sky, and young children couldn't grasp the concept of destruction and death.

Two days before impact, its track would have it passing by our Moon, missing it by just hundreds of miles. There had been some hope against hope that it would, mercifully, end its journey there instead of continuing on to the sparkling blue marble that has been the sanctuary for all life. But that dream was given little chance of success by physicists calculating its speed, approach angle, and proximity to the Moon.

When the day of the Moon bypass arrived, telescopic video of the scene was being shown on screens everywhere. The Moon, rising above the horizon on the daytime side of Earth, could just barely be seen in the early morning sunlit sky. Soon after, a small black spot, undoubtedly Phobos, could be seen racing toward the Moon. It was moving across the screens from right to left, bringing back dreadful memories of the failed rocket attacks in space. The distance separating the two bodies closed rapidly, and when Phobos disappeared behind the Moon, the hope was that it would crash on the dark side, never to be seen again.

Several minutes of agonizing tension ticked by as a puzzled television announcer asked, "How could any god or deity allow something like this to bring an end to all mankind? Makes me wonder if the universe is all just a random occurrence with no creator or guiding force. I'm sorry to sound so irreverent but I...well folks, I'm sorry to report that it's emerging from the left side of the Moon."

Now any thoughts of a dark side rescue were gone and, unlike the dinosaurs of sixty-five million years ago, mankind knew what was coming in just thirteen short hours. A feeling of despair came over all of humanity as the finality of their fate began to be accepted. Seconds later, all eyes turned back to their screens and all ears perked up, expecting more bad news.

The television announcer, speaking in a loud, very excited voice, said, "Wait, something is wrong, or right, or wrong...I'm not sure!...it...it seems to be moving backwards or passing in front of the Moon."

For the next several minutes, all eyes just stared at whatever screen was in front of them until Phobos disappeared behind the Moon once again. It began to sink in that it was, at least for the time being, in orbit around the Moon, having been captured by its meager gravity. Was this going to be a permanent rescue or just another false hope keeping all mankind in suspense wondering if the Earth's gravity might overwhelm the Moon's hold on Phobos, pulling it down onto our world?

The subsequent explanation of the event was that the minuscule deflection produced by the rockets had redirected it just enough that it passed through the Moon's satellite capture zone, and it didn't have enough velocity to escape. A wave of relief washed over billions when it was further announced it had settled into a low altitude, decaying type orbit that would have it crash into the Moon in less than a year. In a way, it had come full circle, suffering a similar fate had it remained in orbit around Mars.

It had been an epic twenty-three-year journey, having first been knocked out of orbit around Mars, redirected by Saturn's slingshot effect, diverted by a close encounter with Haley's Comet, deflected by impact rockets, and captured by the Moon's gravity. To the people of Earth, this was a glorious outcome to the random billiards game at work in the universe.

Phobos was large enough that, on a moonlit night, people delighted in seeing it dart across the surface of the Moon with the naked eye. Scientists, on the other hand, saw it as a remarkable opportunity for research. Just a tantalizing quarter of a million miles away was raw, exposed material that could supply answers to some of the mysteries of the cosmos. To traverse that distance, NASA was directed to put together a plan to send a manned vehicle to Phobos. Getting there wouldn't be difficult, but time was short because of its ultimate fate.

Phobos circumnavigated the Moon in just over forty minutes, far less than the eight hours it took when it was a satellite of its previous captor. Its twenty minutes spent on the visible side proved to be enough time for observations to confirm that the comet had, indeed, landed in Stickney Crater. The heat of the impact had melted the ice and the coldness of space refroze it, forming the now officially named Stickney Lake, confirming yet another one of Mr. Nichols's theories.

CHAPTER 15
THE SHUTTLE

Sara and Ryan had prepared for the impact like everyone else but had never given into hopelessness. Amy practically tackled her friend when she realized she had been right about Phobos not being an instrument of doom.

"Are you some kind of wizard?" Amy demanded.

Sara laughed at her and said, "I was puzzled when the most inspiring event in my life was threatening to ultimately be my maker. I knew there had to be more to it than that. I was supposed to be a scientist. I had always known that. My telescope, the comet, Mr. Nichols, meeting Ryan, all of it has led me here on this path. There was a reason behind this chaos. Phobos is my world. I wasn't going to give that up. People looked at me with pity, overlooking my determination and assuming I was in denial. But I was right. I'm not sure how I knew it, but I'm not going to question it."

For the expedition, NASA required two astronauts, test pilots, an expert geologist, and someone very knowledgeable about Phobos. To pick from hundreds of qualified individuals, they organized a selection committee located at the Kennedy Space Center in Florida.

Jeff Stark, still working there as an astronomer, wasn't on the committee himself but learned they were seeking someone acquainted with Phobos. He looked over the list of prospects and was surprised that Sara Arness's name wasn't on it. Years ago he learned that she, like him, had witnessed the comet impact event live. He had read her book and always looked forward to reading the latest comprehensive technical paper she authored as an astronomer at the Morris Observatory.

He approached a colleague named Gavin who was a member of the committee and told him he would like to nominate someone who was familiar with Phobos. Gavin told him they already had several self-proclaimed Phobos experts right there at the space center. Jeff pressed, "At least let me tell you about this person."

Gavin reluctantly said, "Alright, go ahead."

Jeff informed him that, "Her name is Sara Arness, and I've been following her career for some time because we may hire her someday. As a practicing astronomer, she's a member in good standing of the International Astronomical Union. Her book, *Phobos The Lost Moon*, is widely considered to be the quintessential volume on the subject, and she is one of the few people to have actually see the comet impact live."

Gavin said, "We're really leaning toward someone from right here in the lab."

Jeff, suspecting there might be some politics involved, asked, "Well would you at least let me make a presentation about her to the committee?"

An obviously uneasy Gavin contemplated Jeff's request for a few seconds and finally relented with, "Alright. Come to the next meeting and make your pitch."

After Jeff's presentation, the committee unanimously voted her onto the list.

He called Sara at the observatory, and when she answered, he said, "Hello, this Jeff Stark at NASA."

Sara remembered him and was astonished to hear from him after all these years. Thinking he might want to offer her a job, she just said, "Mr. Stark, how are you?"

"I'm fine, and I just gave a presentation about you," he disclosed.

A suspicious Sara asked, "'A presentation? About what?"

"It was about your intimate knowledge and book about Phobos and your widely read technical papers." Now she was convinced a job offer was coming. He continued, "The presentation was given to the selection committee for the expedition to Phobos. It convinced them to put you on their list of possible candidates."

Sara was astounded; she hadn't even dared to fantasize about something like this and finally got out, "I don't know what to say. I don't have any astronaut training, and there must be more accomplished people than me."

He reassured her, "Things like training can easily be taken care of, and I think you have as good a chance as anyone on the list to end up on the team. They have to make their selections soon, so if you're okay with this, I wouldn't make any long-term plans."

A now dazed Sara said, "I can't think of anything to say except of course I would accept. Are-are they looking for a geologist too?"

"Yes, I think they are," he replied. She reminded him her husband Ryan is a geologist. Jeff said, "Oh yeah, I remember him. I'll mention it to Tom Jeffords. He might want to look into his qualifications."

That ended the call, and Sara just sank into her chair with previously unimaginable thoughts swimming in her head.

Ryan was out of town on a research project that week, but she couldn't wait to call him. He answered with, "Hello darling, how are you?"

She said, "I have some news that—"

He interrupted, "Sara, I'm on the side of a mountain digging in the dirt, can it possibly wait?"

She said, "Okay, but I'll be holding my breath the entire time."

He laughed and said, "Thanks, I'll call you later. Sorry, babe."

Jeff Stark, in the meantime, had tracked down Tom Jeffords and asked if he recalled Ryan and Sara Arness. Tom said, "Sure, a couple of young scientists that were through here several years ago."

Jeff went on, "Well Ryan could very well be a candidate for the Phobos geology position."

Tom said, "I definitely remember him, but I have no idea what he's doing now. I'll look into it."

When Ryan got back to his hotel room that evening, he immediately called Sara, who answered by letting out a big breath and saying, "Ah, I can finally breathe again."

He said, "Boy, you're in a fun mood today."

She said, "That's because I got a call today from, of all people, Jeff Stark. Remember him?"

He said, "Sure, Kennedy Space Center, right?"

She boasted, "Yep, and he told me I was on the list of people being considered for the Phobos excursion."

In a voice almost an octave higher than usual, he asked, "What? How did that come about?"

"He read my book and reads my papers, so he thought I might be a fit. I reminded him that you're a geologist, and he was going to mention you to Tom Jeffords," she said proudly.

Ryan said, "Well nobody has called me, and do you really think either of us would actually be picked?"

Sara sighed, "Not likely, but we can dream."

After investigating for a couple of days, Tom Jeffords found out Ryan had become a recognized expert in the field of planetary geology, was a member of the Planetary Geology Society of America and was the head of a university's geology department. He also learned that Ryan's paper was recognized as the definitive answer as to why the rockets hadn't deflected Phobos.

Convinced that he would be a viable candidate, Tom put together a presentation for the committee. Several of the committee members were already aware of Ryan's work and convinced the others he should be on the list. Tom called the university to inform Ryan but was told he was in Montana doing some in-the-field research. He emailed instead, notifying Ryan about being placed on the list and asking, if picked for the mission, would he accept it.

Late that night, Ryan, glad to be back in his hotel room after a long, exhausting day of geological prospecting cleaning up, had a room service dinner and opened his laptop hoping for an email from Sara. No such luck, so he zeroed in on one from kennedyspacecenter.org. He immediately responded to Tom Jeffords' email, thanking him and saying he was honored to be on the list and certainly would accept a spot on the team.

It was immensely flattering for this one-time B- student to even be on a list of candidates for such a crucial mission. He knew Sara would probably be asleep by now but really wanted to call and tell her. Then remembering how thrilled she was about her own selection, he decided to save it until he got home, giving her a few more days to gloat before stealing some of the glory.

For Sara, the only good thing about Ryan going out into the field was the reunion when he got home. This time it was going to be especially sweet because they could talk about her being selected. When Ryan did get home, he waited until Rachel was tucked in and asleep before saying, "I've got something to tell that you may or may not be thrilled about."

She said, "I'll let you know that when you tell me whatever it is."

He said, "Well you were so excited about being selected, I didn't want to burst your bubble with this."

Sara, bewildered by this unusual statement from Ryan, said, "Sweetheart, I don't need the preamble, just tell me."

"Alright, two days after you were put on the list, so was I," he told her almost apologetically.

She said, "So you're on the list to be the geologist on the mission and you thought that telling me might 'harsh my mellow' as they say."

"Uh, yeah, that's it," he admitted."

She said, "That's so sweet, Ryan. I love you. It must have been agony keeping that to yourself until now."

"It was!"

That night they stayed up for hours running through every possible scenario and all the science fiction movie plots they could think of. Next day it was back to reality.

It was less than a week later when, at home one evening, they both got an email from NASA at the same time. Ryan was hesitant to open his immediately, but Sara coaxed him on, saying, "Come on, we'll both do it at the same time...1...2...3...go." Double clicks right in sync popped open their emails.

Sara's read, "At this time you are the top candidate and will be selected, pending a physical examination, for the position as the Phobos authority on NASA's excursion to Phobos. To accept, please respond ASAP."

Ryan's similarly read, "At this time you are the top candidate and will be selected, pending a physical examination, for the position as the planetary geologist on NASA's excursion to Phobos. To accept, please respond ASAP."

They looked at each other in startled shock and were too overwhelmed to speak.

Ryan finally said, "We've got to answer these right away!"

When she was finished, Sara smiled from ear to ear, thinking somehow Mr. Nichols must have had something to do with this.

The top candidates for the other two positions on NASA's four-man team also immediately accepted the impossible to turn down offer. They would all train for a few months at Cape Canaveral in Florida.

Ryan and Sara were immediately given time off from their jobs and grandparents and Amy gladly volunteered to care for Rachel. Within days, Ryan and Sara relocated to the cape. The other team members, Martin Caldwell and Tom Dunning, were already there when they arrived.

They were all given temporary housing near the base and joined up for dinner that first night. The entire evening was spent exchanging stories on how they came to be sitting at this table. Martin and Tom were dumbfounded while listening as Sara told her story about seeing the comet when she was just nine-years-old. She remembered every detail of that night even though it was two decades ago. They talked about their thoughts when it seemed sure that life on Earth was going to end. They had all shared the same feeling that something totally unforeseen would take place. There was a camaraderie among them and electricity in the air at that dinner table.

They talked for hours about Phobos and the upcoming space trip. Both Martin and Tom were air force test pilots and had completed astronaut training. Since Sara and Ryan wouldn't be required to pilot any vehicle, they would only need specialized training here in Florida and zero gravity training at the Johnson Space Center in Houston, Texas. With Ryan being a planetary geologist and Sara an astronomer, they made an ideal team for such a mission. If only Amy could hear the 'nerd talk' now.

A shuttle had been selected as the best vehicle for the mission. None of the four crew members had ever been in space and for the test pilots in the group, a shuttle would be easy to learn to fly and land. The shuttle is divided into three sections: a cockpit, which was environmentally controlled, an air lock into the cargo bay, and the cargo bay itself.

A PLM (Phobos Lander Module), the vehicle that would be used to actually land on Phobos, would be stored in the cargo bay and brought back to Earth after the mission. The PLM had a cockpit large enough for three occupants and a small rear area with a hatch to exit the vehicle. Being stored in the cargo bay meant no precise docking would have to be learned, just a delicate latching maneuver when guiding it back into the bay. During the months the crew was training, a retired shuttle was being reconditioned and brought back into service.

Their physical training included some brief calisthenics and a three-mile morning run. Sara and Ryan had to learn to walk in magnetic boots since Phobos has a high iron content but very low gravity. The boots would keep them from drifting off the surface and give them Earth-like traction during their exploratory hike. The PLM would be secured to the ground with magnetic pods.

The shuttle, located at the Kennedy Space Center, was appropriately named Phobos1. It would travel to the Moon, get close to Phobos, and stay in synchronous orbit with it. Later it would eject the lander into space and continue in orbit around the Moon while waiting for the lander to return.

Martin would stay in the shuttle while everyone else rode the lander to the surface. The plan was to land it about five hundred yards from Stickney Crater. Ryan and Sara would then walk to the lake, collecting soil and rock samples along the way. Once there, Ryan would get ice samples and Sara would take video and record her observations. She thought it absolutely ironic she was going to observe Phobos up close instead of through Nexter's eyepiece.

Flying the shuttle was Martin's job but they all had to learn the controls in case of unforeseen incidents. Tom and Ryan spent a lot of time planning how to secure the ice collected from Stickney Lake. After many experiments, they concluded the best way was to preserve it in liquid nitrogen, which is -340 degrees.

Sara wasn't too interested in this aspect of the trip but discovered an available telescope at the training facility. She nicknamed it Nexter 2.0 and spent a lot of her spare time viewing 'her,' now up close, moon. Much of Tom's time was spent in the simulator practicing how to fly the PLM, concentrating mostly on landing and the re-docking maneuver back into the cargo bay. Martin was learning the intricacies of handling the shuttle. The months of training went by quickly, and on one of their morning runs during the final week, they could all see the shuttle being moved to the launch pad.

When departure time came, there was no fear, only excitement, among them as they suited up for take-off. They rode in the transporter to the shuttle, cheering as it finally struck them the time was actually here. The technicians strapped them into their seats, closed the hatch, and they were on their own.

Eyes filled with excitement stared straight ahead into the sky above them. "We're about to be up there," someone whispered.

They had a long check list to go through before take-off. When finished, the countdown was set to five minutes. It seemed like an eternity to them, but finally they heard the classic, "Five, four, three, two, one, and ignition!"

The shuttle began to shake as the engines fired, and they could feel it start to rise. As it roared skyward, the G forces began to push them deep into their seats. The first stage broke away with a bang, and the second stage came to life. They were out of the Earth's gravity in less than ten minutes and on their way to the two moons.

CHAPTER 16
THE MISSION

The rocket engines eventually shut down, the G forces subsided, and they were beginning to experience weightlessness.

"Someone's going to be living their dream," Ryan joked.

"Uh, yeah. I'm not sure if you've noticed but we're all in space right now," Sara teased back.

The four of them laughed. The laughter turned into cackling, and the cackling turned into cheers of excitement. After a while, they realized nothing could have prepared them for the reality of space. So empty. So quiet. Infinity took on a whole new meaning.

Day one of the 240,000-mile trip was spent mostly checking the status of the shuttle after the violent force of the take-off. Tom put on his helmet and went through the air lock and into the bay to check the PLM. When he returned to the cockpit, everyone had settled down and was experimenting with the joys of weightlessness. Eating for the first time in this environment required some unusual dexterity. Surprisingly, at the end of the day, without any nighttime darkness in space, they all had a relatively normal sleep cycle.

Day two started with more checks and a lot of communication with ground control. Looking out the port, they got their first uninterrupted view of the Earth, which was continually shrinking in size. Conversely, the Moon was getting larger, which served to heighten their anticipation, but the professionalism of this group kept their pulse rates under control. Now there was time for some meaningless conversation, including Sara's usual witty, humorous, and sometimes thought-provoking remarks. They had some laughs, which had a calming effect, but sleep was less readily achieved that night.

Waking up for day three saw the Moon beginning to dominate the view out of the port. The dark spot occasionally darting across the surface of the Moon was undoubtedly Phobos. That day they ate meals, completed their required duties, and eagerly waited for the shuttle to dispense with the rest of the miles between them and their objective.

When they got close, Martin's first task was to get the shuttle lined up in the same orbital path as Phobos. Not at exactly the same distance off the Moon's surface or it could collide with them on one of its passes.

It was several minutes before the ex-moon came whizzing by at a safe distance below them. What followed was like a super high speed NASCAR race as Martin chased it around the Moon before skillfully getting in sync with its speed and maneuvering to less than a half mile above it. He said, "Well there it is. Doesn't seem like much of a menace just floating out there."

Ryan weighed in with, "May not look like much but traveling at a few miles per second it possesses the force of an object thousands of times its size."

From this height, they could make out some of the smaller details on the surface. It was a mind-numbing sight, even for this experienced group. The reality of where they were and what they were about to do rose to the peak of their consciousness. This was it, what they had trained for, and they were ready. It was an especially poignant moment for Sara. She and Phobos were old friends.

They spent the rest of that day observing it up close, taking radiation readings, and picking a suitable landing spot for the PLM. Everything had to go just right because, with the quickly decaying orbit of this errant body, they would only be able to make this one landing.

After they all spent several, mostly unsuccessful, hours trying to get a night's sleep, Sara, Ryan, and Tom eagerly put on their helmets, went through the shuttle's air lock chamber, got into the PLM, and settled into their seats. When they were strapped in and ready, Tom radioed Martin, "Any time now."

Martin said, "Stay safe down there," as he opened the bay doors.

When they were fully opened, Tom had the computer release the latches that held the PLM in place. As soon as it displayed "RELEASED," he fired up the rockets. There was no sound as they lifted out of the bay into the dark, quiet, solitude of space. Tom kept it in manual control mode, using this opportunity to get accustomed to flying it for real.

The trip down to Phobos took several minutes but to the crew, time was inconsequential. Tom was concentrating on guiding the lander, and Sara and Ryan were captivated by the scenery out of the view port. For a moment, Sara's thoughts drifted back over the events that led her to this point. It all seemed so surreal. Would standing on Phobos be more exciting than the trip to the planetarium that had awakened her interest in astrology? Or when she saw the comet collision with Nexter or Mr. Nichols interest in tutoring her? A sudden bump snapped her out of the past and back into the present. They had touched down, and Tom had activated the magnetic pods. She would know the answer soon.

They were located, as planned, about a half mile from the crater. They just sat there for a few seconds in awe of where they were. The onboard computer checked the iron content of the surface and automatically adjusted the holding force of the magnetic pods. Next it displayed a seven and sounded a beep. The seven would be the setting for the magnetic boots.

Sara and Ryan made their way back to the hatch area and buckled up their boots. Sara pondered, "Could you imagine just floating in space completely alone, with nothing to hold you down? No control over where you went and no matter where you looked, just darkness?"

Ryan replied, "You really know how to settle someone's nerves, let me tell you," as he struggled with his boots, his hands shaking from sheer excitement.

They undid the latches on the hatch, and with one last look at each other, Ryan pulled it open.

Sara said, "I'll go first."

She clicked on the magnetics for her boots, grabbed the outside handrail, pulled herself through the hatch opening, and swung down to the surface. The boots held her firmly on the ground, and after one apprehensive step, she was relieved she didn't sink into the 'void.' She couldn't believe it. She was actually standing on Phobos. An impossible dream, now a reality, and yes it was the most exciting of all the events leading up to this moment.

She called up to Ryan, "It's okay, come on down…lets go for a walk."

Ryan turned on his boots and swung down next to her. As they started walking, there was no sensation of ground motion even though it was rotating at several miles per second. At one point in the rotation, they could see the moon over one shoulder and the Earth over the other. A breathtaking sight that gave them a feeling they could never quite find the right words to explain.

Before them lay a rocky, colorless terrain with very little dust, so no matter how hard they tried, they couldn't leave any footprints. They had hoped to follow in the footsteps, pun intended as they would always say, of Neil Armstrong. However, it looked like that wasn't going to happen.

It turned out to be more than just a leisurely stroll to Stickney Lake because it took them a while to get used to the magnetic boots. The reality of walking in them here was quite different from what they had experienced while practicing on Earth. During their uphill trudge to the edge of the frozen lake, Ryan collected rock and soil samples and Sara took video. When they finally got there, Ryan radioed Tom and between gasps for air told him, "The walk was tougher than we thought."

"Yeah, I can tell," Tom laughed.

In front of them lay the once empty crater, now almost completely filled with ice that was probably billions of years old. Unlike a flat, smooth ice-skating rink, its surface was rough and dotted with dark areas most likely from the dust and dirt contained in the comet's ice, which gave them their nickname of dirty snowballs. The lake, which had looked almost completely round from Earth, now showed spikes of ice, like horizontal icicles, sticking out of the shoreline where the water had squirted out before being refrozen. It had the look of a starburst or a giant crown of thorns.

Sara kept taking video as Ryan took the last few steps down to the pointed end of one of these icicles and started to gently chip at it with the pick to gather samples. While Sara was taking a left to right panoramic video scan of the lake's surface, she spotted something sticking out of the ice that looked out of place.

"Ryan, I see something out there that looks interesting. It's about three hundred yards straight out."

"Okay, I'll come take a look when I'm done here," he replied.

Sara finished the complete scan and recorded several verbal notes before Ryan was finished. When he walked back up to her, she handed him the camera and he zoomed in on the object saying, "You're right, it's very interesting and seems to be kind of triangular shaped. I wish we could go check it out, but the surface of the lake isn't magnetic. I'd hate to be the one to test your theory of what it's like to be stuck floating in space. Let's take some more video, get back to the lander, and find out what ground control wants us to do."

They took a slightly different course back to the lander, hoping to find more items for the nitrogen container. Having become comfortable with the magnetic boots and being exhilarated from their exotic find, they even tried to skip, but the boots just wouldn't allow it.

Back in the lander, they were more excited than when they left. Ryan stowed all his valuable samples in the liquid nitrogen tank before they went back into the cockpit. When Tom saw Sara's video, he said, "Looks like something manmade or maybe even alien made. This could be as important as Phobos itself. Let's transmit the video to Martin."

They waited for quite a while with hearts pounding in anticipation before Martin finally contacted them saying, "It wasn't recognized on the ground as anything NASA had ever sent into space, and they think it could be some kind of foreign or alien capsule. They're very interested in it and said if we have a plan, to go ahead, but don't jeopardize the overall mission."

Tom asked, "Okay, anyone have a plan?"

Sara, who had been formulating something while waiting for the go ahead, spoke up saying, "How about this? Since we can't walk out onto the ice, maybe we can somehow use the lander to get to it. Tom, you won't be able to use the magnetic pods, but do you think you could hover this thing over whatever that is?"

Tom smiled, "Well it never came up in simulator training, but I'm willing to give it a try. What do you have in mind?"

Sara said, "Well it looked like there was about a yard or two sticking out of the ice, and there must be more underneath, or it would have floated away. One of us can drop a cable around it, tether ourselves to the cable, and chip away at the ice. If it's possible to get it loose, we can tow it back to the shuttle."

They all considered this option for just a few seconds before Ryan said, "Well it was very easy to chip the ice with the pick, so that might work. What do you think, Tom?"

He said, "Astronauts have been doing space walks with a tether for a long time, and this wouldn't be much different. So I'm okay with it. The only problem is we don't have a lot of extra fuel, so I won't be able to hover for very long."

Tom contacted Martin again to ask if he thought there was room in the shuttle bay to hold it. Martin suggested they get back to him when they get a better reading of its size. Then after a deep breath, Tom said, "Let's do this…It'll be just like flying a helicopter but with almost no gravity...should be interesting."

Ryan added, "I've practiced flying a helicopter in a simulator, so maybe I can help you keep it steady."

Sara perked up and said, "Since you two will be busy keeping this thing hovering, I'll take the spacewalk."

When everyone was strapped in, Tom released the magnetic pods, fired a short rocket burst on very low power, and the lander jumped off the surface. When it got up to about ten yards, he fired other rockets to stop it from going any higher and start it moving toward the crater. In a short time they were at the edge of the lake, and Tom tipped the nose of the lander down toward the surface to be able to locate the object through the view port.

Sara yelled, "There it is, off to the left. It does looks like some kind of capsule. If it's not one of ours, maybe it's from some far-off galaxy!"

This was better than Christmas morning for Sara.

Tom, still learning how to hover using rocket bursts, maneuvered the lander closer to the object and struggled to keep up with the exact rotation speed of the ice below him. When he got close, he kept the lander hovering off to one side, just a couple yards above the surface of the ice.

Ironically, holding this steady position made them a stationary satellite of Phobos. Sara took the pick and the cable, made her way back to the hatch, and pulled it open. The object was still a little too far off to the right, so she directed Tom saying, "Two yards to the right."

Tom fired a very small rocket burst while Ryan watched the surface to see how far they had moved. Ryan said, "One yard too far, back up." The next rocket burst put the hatch right over the top of the object.

Sara yelled, "Hold it right there!"

Tom said, "Easier said than done...give me a couple of minutes to see if I can keep this thing in one place." He asked Ryan to pick a spot on the ice as a reference and tell him how he was doing. The lander was rocking slightly left to right and slightly up and down, but Tom soon learned to steady it. When he got completely comfortable with his ability to control it, he said in his best self-assured voice, "Okay, Sara you can go now."

She made a loop in the end of the cable and, much like a rodeo performer with a lasso, used what little gravity there was to drop it right around the top of the object. She attached the other end of the cable to a handle on the outside of the lander and attached her tether to the cable with a rock climber's carabineer. She advised Tom, "The cable is hooked up...I've left some slack to give you a little leeway." She teased Tom and Ryan saying, "I'll be right back, so don't leave without me." Tom laughed, but Ryan didn't think it was funny. She gave a slight pull on the cable and just floated out the opening. Another tug and she actually bumped into whatever it was.

Being up close, Sara could see it was shaped like an hourglass with a ring around the narrow part in the middle. Somewhat over a yard in length was sticking out of the ice, and she decided that if it's symmetrically shaped, there's probably another yard or so below the surface. She got into a comfortable position and took a full swing at the ice with the pick.

As soon as the pick struck the ice, she was reminded of Isaac Newton's third law of motion, which states, "For every action, there is an equal and opposite reaction." With almost no gravity, she was rocketed back up the cable and almost back into the hatch. Sara thought to herself, *Strike one.* Pulling herself back down the cable, she made sure to get a good grip around the narrow waist area of the object before taking another swing.

Just as Ryan had said, the ice chipped away quite easily, so she decided to chip in one spot to see how deep it was embedded in the ice. With every swing, the reaction tried to send her back up the cable. It took only a few swings to make an opening big enough to reach in with her glove. She reached down to the submerged part and could feel it probably was symmetrical, so her yard or so guess was accurate. Now that she had a good sense of its overall shape and size, capsule did seem like a fitting description. She asked Tom to contact Martin and tell him it's about three yards long and about one yard in diameter.

She worked her way around the base with the pick, and every blow sent chips of ice flying up and floating away. Before long she had much of it exposed but realized she might not get it completely free before the lander got low on fuel. She relayed her doubt to Ryan, who said, "Keep chipping for now. I'll check the fuel and talk to Tom. Incidentally Martin says it will fit in the bay." A short time later Ryan answered back saying, "Sara, we are getting low on fuel, but Tom thinks the lander may have enough thrust to pull it out the rest of the way. Want to give it a try?"

"Better than leaving it here," Sara replied.

She slid up to the hatch, disconnected herself from the cable, got inside, and said, "Okay, Tom, I'm in."

As soon as he fired the rockets, the cable got taut, the capsule popped out of the ice, and the recoil caused the lander to roll violently to one side. Tom quickly got it leveled out again with more rocket bursts, but as he did, the door to the hatch tried to swing shut, hitting the air tank on Sara's back, knocking her through the hatch. Now, without her tether hooked up, she was just helplessly wandering off into space.

Ryan's first instinct was to ask her if she came through that turbulence alright.

She responded in an amazingly calm voice saying, "I'm okay, but I'm outside the lander testing my theory about floating in space."

He strained to see out the view port, spotting her floating in space about five yards out and drifting farther away. He bolted back to the hatch area. Looking out, he could see her now about fifteen yards away and steadily getting farther and farther out of reach. The capsule was free floating but still connected to the dangling cable.

Ryan anxiously called out, "Tom, Sara's in real trouble here. Rotate to about three o'clock and let me know when you can see her."

It only took Tom a few seconds to comprehend what was going on, so, as Ryan requested, he fired some small rocket bursts to get the lander to rotate. When she was in view he said, "I see her. I'll start moving toward her." Just as the PLM began to move in her direction, a buzzer started to beep. He glanced at the Fuel Control Screen on the computer, which was blinking LOW FUEL...LOW FUEL...LOW FUEL. He was forced to tune it out, needing all his concentration to negotiate the distance between him and Sara. It would be a delicate, tactical maneuver to match her acceleration while at the same time being careful not to bump into her, which could propel her off in the opposite direction, maybe forever. All while using up precious fuel.

Tom increased the speed of the lander in small increments, creeping closer and closer to her. A terrified Ryan was calling out the distance between him and Sara, "Twenty yards. Fifteen yards. Ten yards." Tom then used rocket blasts to slow the closing speed.

When they were close enough, Ryan reached out as far as he could and tried to grab onto Sara's space suit. Just as he touched her, the lander suddenly rolled several degrees clockwise. Ryan looked out to see the cable had gotten taut again.

"I should cut that damn thing loose," Ryan grumbled.

Sara begged, "Ryan, please don't do that yet. Let Tom take another crack at it."

As Tom started the whole procedure over again, Ryan pulled the capsule up and cinched the cable to the lander. The second attempt went much smoother, and when it was as close to her as Tom dared, he asked, "How's that?"

Ryan, leaning out of the hatch as far as he could, called back, "Just one more yard."

That last move caused Ryan and Sara to actually collide with each other, but he had managed to grab the belt on her suit. He pulled her into the hatch, and after a relieving suit-to-suit hug, Sara said, "How about that? I was almost the one to experience my theory about being stranded in space." Her tone was almost blasé, but a frightened look lingered on her face.

They closed the hatch and made their way back into the cockpit. When they got strapped into their seats, they noticed the Fuel Control Screen blinking LOW FUEL...LOW FUEL.

Sara commented, "I wondered what that beeping noise was in my earpiece."

The screen was indicating 5.1 minutes of rocket burn time remaining.

Tom pulled up the auto pilot screen and selected 'FLIGHT PATH TO SHUTTLE RENDEZVOUS.' The onboard computer, knowing the exact location of the orbiting shuttle and the current rotational position of Phobos, calculated the take-off time, angle, and acceleration needed to meet up with the shuttle. It displayed twenty-three seconds to take-off, 3.7 minutes of rocket burn time, twelve minutes total travel time. Tom, not wanting to use any more fuel for hovering, just let the PLM float while waiting out the twenty-three seconds.

Ryan asked Tom if he thought the remaining 1.4 minutes of burn time that would be left after rendezvous would be enough to get in perfect sync with the speed of the shuttle and fit the PLM into the cargo bay. Tom replied,

"With no unnecessary corrections, and if that thing strapped to the side doesn't give me any problems, it'll be as close as I ever want to get. Maybe too close." With that, Tom set the computer on Auto Pilot mode.

They all sat there waiting out the rest of the twenty-three seconds before the rockets fired, pinning them into their seats and leaving the doomed one-time Mars moon behind forever. Precisely at the 3.7-minute mark, the burn stopped, and they were on a perfect glide path to meet up with Martin and the shuttle. There was no panic among the crew in the lander, just quiet hope.

Martin, aware of their plight, had opened the cargo bay doors early in anticipation of Tom having only one shot at getting it inside. Just before the twelve minute mark, the Auto Pilot screen alerted, '11.3 SECOND BURN FOR SHUTTLE SPEED SYNCHRONIZATION.' This brought the PLM right above the bay doors, traveling at almost exactly the same speed as the shuttle. The Fuel Control Screen indicated 1.21 minutes of burn time remaining.

Fitting the PLM into the cargo bay was like threading a needle—a maneuver Tom had performed many times in the simulator but never under these conditions and never with a constant beep in his earpiece. As he flipped it back into manual control mode, he said a little silent prayer. When he grabbed the controls, decades of test pilot experience kicked in and any pressure he felt faded away. He fired a series of short rocket burns getting it lined up and lowered it into the bay as Ryan called out the remaining burn time.

Just as he was about to settle it back into the latches, Sara warned him a piece of the cable was blocking one of them. Tom uncharacteristically swore, "That damn thing's going to get us all killed."

He rolled the lander slightly clockwise, and Sara yelled, "That's got it."

Ryan alerted, "Nine seconds, Tom."

It took all of that to get it settled into the latches, and just when the computer indicated 'LOCKED,' the Fuel Control Screen displayed 'FUEL EXPENDED.' The beep that had been annoying them all this time finally went silent.

Martin closed the bay doors, and Tom, Ryan, and Sara sat in silence for several seconds, shedding the emotions built up over the last few minutes. Sara broke the silence, in her usual nonchalant way, saying, "Well that was fun...let's get the hell out of this thing."

Being in a weightless environment, it was kind of like swimming out of the PLM and into the shuttle's air lock chamber. When the chamber was filled with oxygen, they could finally take-off their helmets and make their way into the cockpit, where Martin sheepishly said, "Welcome back...so how was the trip?" That started a flood of stories from all three that he heard over and over again for the next 240,000 miles.

Just before they were going to breach Earth's atmosphere, Ryan went back through the air lock and into the bay to detach the object from the PLM and firmly attach the cable to a handle in the bay so it wouldn't be bouncing around during re-entry. He noticed there was still some Stickney ice stuck to it that, unfortunately, would be melted off when they landed. He had Martin notify ground control about this.

Martin piloted the shuttle through re-entry and a skillful touchdown, which brought back the familiar tug of gravity. When it came to a stop, they could see a ground crew already waiting on the tarmac in full protective gear. They were bringing out a crane to lift the object out of the bay and bring it into the lab right there on the base. A different crew would take care of the PLM and the container of liquid nitrogen holding Ryan's samples. Tom noticed there was a lot more security around than usual.

Because of the uniqueness of their mission, as soon as the shuttle was completely shut down, they all removed their space suits and deposited them in the air lock. Ryan and Sara did the same with their magnetic boots. Furthermore, when they departed the shuttle, they were to enter the complex through the medical quarantine door.

When they stepped off the end of the ramp onto solid ground, they all had mixed emotions. Glad to be back safe but dismayed their adventure was over. Sara had the added feeling of nostalgia knowing Phobos would soon succumb to the Moon's gravity and be out of her life forever.

CHAPTER 17
THE ESCAPE

The shuttle was sitting on the tarmac with the bay doors still closed when the ground crew entered the cockpit, headed through the airlock, and opened the air-tight door leading into the bay.

The crew chief, sticking to strict protocol, directed the other members not to enter yet as he cautiously stepped in with a Geiger counter. Not knowing what to expect with some kind of alien craft aboard, he took a cursory look around and then stood in silence for a couple of minutes just listening for any sound. The lack of any movement or noise made it comforting enough for him to approach the PLM and begin taking radiation readings. After going all the way around it and not registering any dangerous levels, he headed for the capsule.

It was still attached to the cable, skillfully dropped around it by Sara, and had the appearance of a giant silver hourglass lying on its side. It seemed to have come through the return trip without any obvious damage. Being hesitant to get too close, he slowly walked up to it with the Geiger counter held at arm's length. The needle barely moved off zero. He noticed a small pool of liquid on the deck just to the left of the capsule. This had to be the melted Stickney ice Martin had warned them about. When it didn't register any radioactivity, he motioned his crew to come in and get to work.

When the crew got inside the bay, they just stood in a kind of hypnotic fascination staring at this mysterious device possibly made by beings of superior intelligence in some far reaches of the universe. Finally one member broke the spell and walked up to check if it was magnetic—it was not. Another used a digital stethoscope to listen for internal sounds—there were none. A third collected the melted ice with a stainless-steel suction gun that resembled a turkey baster.

They removed the cable and wrapped lifting straps around it.

When the bay doors were opened, the crane was brought over, and the straps attached to its hook. As soon as it started to be lifted, the crane's scale measured it at just over four hundred pounds. The two hundred or so yards to the lab was traversed over several agonizingly slow minutes. The entire time the crane was literally surrounded by security. When it got to the large overhead door to the lab, it was gently set down into a cradle that had been hastily constructed during the shuttle's return trip.

As had been reported from the shuttle, it was a perfect hourglass shape with a narrow waist about one foot in diameter. It was almost nine feet in overall length, and both ends were oval shaped and about four feet wide. The type of excitement Sara had felt stepping onto Phobos now filled the engineers who were assigned to learn the secrets of this alien craft. They were all wearing protective gear because their first concern was biosafety. They instructed the chief to isolate the protective gear of anyone involved with it. That included the spacesuits of the crew, the protective gear of anyone conducting the move, and anything else that had contact with the shuttle or the capsule. Before any attempt was made to discover its secrets, the entire surface of the capsule was swabbed, and the samples were tested right there in the lab. Within a few hours, they were relieved to learn it was bio free.

It was clear nothing could be learned until they could breach its outer shell. The first examination revealed no openings or any other obvious ways to get inside. The seam around the neck was the only break in the otherwise smooth, shiny, metallic-like skin. Whether it had been delivered by the comet or was hitchhiking aboard Phobos, possibly for eons, it surprisingly showed no signs of wear. More exact measurements revealed none of its dimensions lined up with US Standard, British Imperial, International Metric, or any other known measurement system.

Attempts to examine its interior with x-rays or other types of scans proved fruitless, and cruder methods like drilling or cutting with a torch couldn't even scratch its surface. Whatever it was made of thwarted all their efforts to crack its outer layer. By the end of the day, they realized further attempts would have to wait until tomorrow, when an expert metallurgist would be on site. The lab was locked down, and the guard was instructed not to enter it that night.

Later that evening, just as the guard had gotten back to his station after making routine rounds, there was a loud noise coming from the far end of the building. He checked all his monitors, but everything looked normal. He hurried down the long hallway in the direction of the noise, checking every room and office until he got to the lab door. He stood there debating whether he should go in, regardless of his orders not to, but decided the noise couldn't be ignored. When he opened the security door, he could feel a rush of air flowing around him and into the lab.

Peering into the darkness, he got an eerie feeling he might have to make a hurried exit. Knowing the security door would automatically close behind him, he jammed his night stick into the hinge to keep it open. Not really knowing what to expect, he unbuckled the strap holding the .45 pistol into its holster and cautiously stepped into the dark, silent lab. He scanned the room with his flashlight, and when it illuminated the cradle built to hold the capsule, he was startled to find it empty.

Following the stream of air led him around a corner to the back wall which now had two five-foot round holes in it. The wall was almost two feet thick and lined with metal screening to prevent external radio interference. Whatever made these holes had cut clean through drywall, metal screening, wood, concrete, and anything else in its way. There was debris all over the floor and scattered on the grass strip outside leading to the empty parking lot. Streetlights and moonlight supplied enough illumination for him to see several hundred yards down the road...there was nothing.

He thought about going through one of the openings to look around outside but decided his footprints might destroy some evidence, and he wasn't too keen about venturing into the dark without any backup. Suddenly a loud screeching noise filled the room. He instinctively ducked, drew his pistol like a Texas cowboy, and scanned the room looking for the source. After a few seconds, he realized it was the alarm set off by the jammed open security door. When he regained his composure, he turned on the lights and explored the rest of the lab, finding nothing else had been disturbed.

The alarm had automatically notified the head of security and the local police. Upon arrival, they locked down the lab and, knowing this wasn't just a simple case of robbery, called in the FBI. All local patrol cars were alerted to be on the lookout for trucks traveling the roads. Helicopters were up searching a one hundred square mile area, and roadblocks were set up on the highways leading out of town. By morning, the lab was crawling with investigators, and when the engineers showed up for work, the yellow crime scene tape alerted them to the fact something serious had happened. The entire space center was shut down and everyone was questioned.

The investigators were baffled as to how anyone could have gotten something as large and heavy as the capsule out of the lab without some heavy-duty equipment like a forklift, but there were no tracks on the grass or in the parking lot. The holes in the wall offered very little in the way of clues and, as the guard told them, other than the empty cradle and those holes, everything else was normal. The head of security told the FBI that, because of the secret nature of the work done in there, they had never considered installing cameras inside the lab.

Police were taking photos and dusting everything for fingerprints. An investigator with 'FBI' in large letters on the back of his jacket was questioning the security chief about the measures they had for entering the lab. The chief responded, "Well, to enter the lab we use iris recognition, where you have to look into a lens just outside the door which scans the iris in your eye and uses it like a fingerprint to identify you. If you are approved, the door will open automatically. There is also a sensor detecting that only one person at a time enters the lab. I honestly don't see how anyone could have pulled this off."

The officer shook his head, asking, "How about when leaving the lab?"

The chief replied, "Since you're already in the lab, we don't eye-scan you again. There's a simple palm scanner where you put your hand against a piece of glass and the door opens. It's just to check who has left and at what time."

The officer said, "I'll need the records of everyone who's been in and out of here for the last twenty-four hours." He went on, "What about those large doors over there?"

The chief explained, "Those doors can only be opened by the head of security. If they get breached, an alarm sounds and all the guards get notified on their walkie-talkies. There was no alarm from that door last night."

CHAPTER 18
SARA'S THEORY

The following morning during breakfast, Sara and Ryan, having been notified about the missing capsule, were having an intense discussion about the events of the previous day.

At some point they were distracted by a news broadcast about some unusual vapor trails in the sky. Unusual in that they were very narrow and had originally started out as just one, continually circling the globe in a north to south direction at supersonic speed. At some point it spawned a second one going east to west. The air force scrambled some planes in an attempt to track down whatever was causing them. But by the time they got up to the suspected altitude, nothing was found, and the trails were beginning to fade. Sara and Ryan hurried outside to get a glimpse of what looked like a giant cross. By the time they got to the lab, the trails had faded away. The vapor trails, along with the missing capsule, were the topics of the day.

Much of their day was spent in debriefing sessions covering the entire mission. As they recounted the events, all seemed so anticlimactic now it was over. There were several interruptions by FBI investigators with questions about the missing capsule.

On their twenty-minute drive back to their temporary housing that evening, they were listening to reports about a sequence of earthquakes occurring around the world. First it was thought to be just an original quake followed by several aftershocks, but as they continued at regular intervals, some ill-omened force was suspected. The initial one had been measured at a very low magnitude of 1.4 on the Richter scale. Then at regular intervals there would be another at a slight increase in magnitude. So far the energy levels have been far too low to be destructive, but if they continued at the current rate, they could eventually wreak havoc on the whole planet. Seismologists couldn't explain them and, curiously enough, couldn't locate their epicenters.

Sara was noticeably quiet for several minutes as they drove along and finally said, "Ryan, I have a really absurd idea about what might be going on here. We need to stop off at Barnes and Noble before we go home."

He asked, "Anything you want to discuss?"

She said, "No, not yet. What I'm thinking is so far-fetched I want to look up something before I even tell you about it."

After Ryan parked the car, they both went into the store, and Sara immediately headed off to the section where she thought she might find the material she was looking for. Ryan looked around nostalgically, recalling the time he worked at Barnes and Noble, when he and Sara first met. He wandered around the store for a while checking if the layout was similar to the one where he worked. He turned down one aisle and found Sara sitting on the floor, surrounded by a stack of books.

He inquired, "Are you done?"

She said, "Almost. Why don't you make one more trip around and come back and get me?"

As soon as they got back in the car, a very excited Sara asked Ryan if he remembered learning about Nikola Tesla.

Ryan said, "Sure, he was an electrical engineer in the early 1900s. I think he worked for Thomas Edison."

Sara said, "He was more than an engineer. He was an electrical genius. He and Edison had a falling out over whether alternating current or direct current was the best way to deliver electricity. Tesla was right about alternating current, and that's what the world uses today."

She continued, "He also did a lot of experimenting with oscillators. You know, things that vibrate at a certain rate or frequency. I just read that he was changing the frequency of one to see if it would get in tune with a wall or something. He would start at a low rate and keep speeding it up little by little until it got in tune with the vibration of the entire building."

Ryan interrupted, "If you recall from physics classes, everything has a resonant frequency where it will vibrate wildly all by itself. It has to be exact. Not too slow, and not too fast."

Sara continued with, "I think Tesla went on to speculate that he could put one on each end of the Earth and cause enough vibration to split it in half."

A confused Ryan asked, "What does all that have to do with us?"

Sara explained, "Well this may sound crazy, but I have a theory that our capsule might have been the very thing we needed when we thought Phobos was going to take us out. Call it kind of a 'planet protector' that can take care of any cosmic body threatening your home planet. Actually I think it's really two capsules connected together.

"Remember, it had a ring around the narrow middle section that the technicians couldn't open? Maybe it could split itself into two parts, with each half having its own propulsion system. Then they could work in unison to deflect, vaporize, or somehow destroy any possible threat to their home planet. If the threat is a large body like the Earth, that couldn't be deflected or vaporized, they could use Tesla's vibration principal, creating earthquakes to put it into resonant frequency and shake itself into small non-lethal pieces.

"These earthquakes may be the capsules hunting for the resonant frequency of the Earth. Current theory doesn't think Tesla was right because Earth has a liquid center, which would absorb the shock wave trying to pass through it. But whoever built this thing is obviously light years ahead of us. Did you hear the reports of UFOs earlier today? Those UFOs might have been the capsules searching for the optimum spots to dive into the Earth's crust and start creating sonic vibrations.

"Eventually, with thousands of gaping cracks, the Earth's crust could no longer contain its solid iron inner core. The entire earth would probably break up and become just a lot of debris destined to orbit around the Sun. So now instead of a 'planet protector,' it's become a 'planet killer.'"

Ryan asked, "So why didn't it destroy the comet or Phobos?"

She speculated, "Possibly, for relatively small bodies, it just deflects them away from a deadly heading and then locks itself together and stays onboard in case it becomes a threat again in the future. But now the capsules find themselves on a large mass and, not knowing how far it is away from the home planet, its artificial intelligence has calculated it could someday be a threat and must be destroyed. Frightening to think that this device was built to save a planet in another galaxy and now we have to stop it from destroying our own, and we don't even know how it works."

Ryan said, "If you're right, we may not have much time to find and stop them."

Sara said, "I have to check my suspicion with one more person."

Ryan quipped, "That would be Mr. Nichols."

Sara called him, and after some thought, he contended, "Your theory seems possible. They could find the resonant frequency by triggering earthquakes that travel in a spherical direction to get around the Earth's liquid center and then measure its effect. As more and more quakes are triggered, the Earth will get closer and closer to resonance. When it's reached, it will begin to bulge and distort and eventually break apart into small pieces.

"They could even have some way of scattering the remaining fragments out into space so they couldn't coalesce back together. Should that happen, the Earth would no longer exist, and the Moon would just continue on its orbit around the Sun. We don't have the technology to do that, but if this thing was created by an advanced civilization in some far-off galaxy, it might be possible. Finding the resonance may take several days. So if you can figure out a way to disable one or both of them, it might stop the whole process. Sorry I have to be the one to confirm your suspicion."

CHAPTER 19
THE SEARCH

Sara called the colonel who had been in charge of their mission and presented her suspicion. At first he was understandably quite skeptical but the more they discussed it, the more he began to see a correlation between what she was saying and what was actually happening.

He finally said, "Let me make a couple of calls, and I'll get right back to you."

Sara nervously paced around the house until the phone rang and the colonel told her, "The White House and the military have been contacted and a worldwide search has begun for ideas on how to locate the epicenters to narrow down the search area."

They were immediately flooded with calls and emails from engineers and scientists from all over the world with ideas on how they could help in the search. One of the most promising came from a Serbian seismologist named Kristof Lalic who told them he was sure he could locate the epicenter of the quakes. In checking his background, they discovered, amazingly, that he is actually a descendant of the late Nikola Tesla. That explained his interest in earthquakes and why he had become an expert at interpreting seismographs, records of the Earth's motion.

They also learned he had just completed a two-year long project developing a computer program that uses global seismograph readings to locate hard to find earthquake epicenters. If the capsules were the source of the quakes, his program may be the solution they were desperately looking for. He would need every country's seismographs for the last few days, and then it would take him several hours to enter all their data into his program. A military jet was dispatched to bring him to the lab.

Getting the seismographs proved to be a politically diplomatic problem because not all countries were convinced that some unproven story about a couple of strange capsules could be the source of the quakes. After some hurried, top-level meetings and prodding, Kristof began to get the data from around the world, and as soon as he arrived at the lab and set up his equipment, he started downloading it all.

It wasn't until late the following morning he got most of what he needed and was able to start his program on its epic search. It ran for hours with no results. Kristof, pacing around the lab and muttering in Serbian, mimicking his late uncle, couldn't discern why his program wasn't yielding any results. He began to suspect the shock waves were traveling in spherical directions around the globe, as Mr. Nichols had speculated. That had to be how the capsules were getting around Earth's liquid center and would also explain why other seismologists couldn't locate the epicenter. He immediately began to update his program to compensate for this new development.

After a lengthy re-write, he sat at his terminal sifting through the results it was displaying on his screen. He knew that waves called P and S cause the most destructive kind of earthquakes and travel at an average speed of about three miles per second. The circumference of the Earth at the equator is about 25,000 miles, so it takes about forty minutes for the waves created at both antipodal (exact polar opposite) locations to meet near the equator. It seemed to be taking the capsules several hours to inject enough vibrations into the ground to cause an earthquake.

Checking the Richter scale reading of the most recent one, his best guess was that it would take about seventy-two more hours for them to find that terminal vibration. All he could do for now was wait for his program to produce enough data so he could locate the epicenters and predict where the capsules might be found.

Populating the lab by now were other seismologists, military personnel, NASA, FBI, and CIA officials, along with Ryan and, of course, Sara, who sat right next to Kristof day and night. A General Tallmadge took over all activity in the lab, but Sara warned him not to disturb Kristof.

To most people, Kristof's data would just look like random numbers scrolling on the screen, but he knows what it all means and was looking for patterns he could interpret to direct him to the epicenters. Sara didn't understand the numbers, but after watching the screen for hours, she began to notice some strange repeating patterns in the background. Kristof and the other seismologists weren't looking for these particular patterns, and she was hesitant to interrupt them and break their concentration.

Eventually she and Kristof took a short break, and Sara worked up the nerve to mention her suspicion. At first he was hesitant to think an untrained person could have actually found anything useful, but he agreed to listen. She said since his program was collecting the vibration frequencies shaking the Earth, maybe what she was seeing, buried within his data, could be some kind of communication between the capsules. This theory caught his attention and that ended their break.

He told the other seismologists what to watch for on his screen as he wrote a program on his laptop to segregate what Sara was seeing from all his accumulated earthquake data. It took him less than an hour to finish the program, and when he ran it, sure enough, a pattern began to emerge.

It appeared to be some kind of code that is foreign or alien to him and all the computer geeks in the lab. Sara called Mr. Nichols again for help with this new development, and he told her the NSA (National Security Agency) has a secret program using quantum computing for code breaking. Secret had little meaning in light of this situation, where the very survival of the Earth hung in the balance. He put Sara in touch with them, and they told her that Blakeley Madison, who heads the Quantum Cryptography team, was the right person for this task. Sara Skyped with Blakeley and explained her suspicion.

Blakeley said, "Send me all your data, and we'll get started."

Now there were two teams racing to come up with the answer on how to find these killers.

Tension around the planet was ramping up at an alarming rate as everyone could see their world literally crumbling around them. It was all happening so fast that only a few of the world's population were aware of the effort going on in the two labs.

Several hours later there was a loud cheer in the lab when Kristof's program displayed the location of the epicenters and predicted where the capsules were with an accuracy of only about +/- fifteen miles. This left a search area of about nine hundred square miles to find the insignificantly small impressions made by the capsules when they dove into the crust.

He could tell they were at exact antipodal locations on the globe. One was in a southeastern Antarctica ice cap at approximately -78° latitude and 106° longitude, and the other one was on the west coast of Greenland, near 78° latitude and 106° longitude.

Standard search methods certainly wouldn't be able to find them in time. NASA said the best way to search areas this large was to use Polar Orbiting Satellites. These satellites operate in special Low Earth Orbits north and south over the Earth's poles. Low orbits allow for much higher resolution video images but cover a smaller area with each orbit. This is ideal for finding small objects in a sea of ice, but since these satellites were not geostationary (in sync with the Earth's rotation), it would take an unknown number of orbital scans to cover the combined 1,800 square miles.

After each scan, a computer would use digital signal processing in an attempt to pinpoint the impressions left by the capsules. If it isn't successful, the whole process starts over with a new scan. Even when they're found, they are in very remote, almost inaccessible parts of the planet usually traveled only by dog sleds and have most likely burrowed down several thousand yards into the Earth's crust.

The situation became even more problematic when it was realized the southernmost capsule was near the Russian research station of Vostok. This area of the Antarctic is called the Southern Pole of Inaccessibility, close to the south geomagnetic pole. This explained why the capsules picked this as one of their antipodal locations. America has a station in Antarctica named McMurdo, but it's almost four hundred miles away from the suspected capsule location, so Russian authorization would be needed to even get near Vostok.

The state department was immediately drafted to contact their Russian counterparts. Their immediate response was although the quakes were coming at regular intervals, they weren't convinced they were being created by some alien capsules. At the moment, they suspected the CIA might be using this opportunity to learn about their work at Vostok.

After all attempts to convince them had failed, the president was called in. The vice president, along with the top members of the state department, joined him in the Oval Office where the famous red phone was used to contact the Russian president. Amongst all the confusion with language translation and distrust, an agreement was eventually worked out where limited access to the Vostak station would be allowed. Their security would monitor our every move.

NASA began their satellite searches as the succession of earthquakes continued to shake the planet more and more. Conditions around the world were reaching a critical state as some areas were slowly crumbling into almost unrecognizable landscapes. The earthquakes had created a shift in the movement of the Earth's tectonic plates, bringing about unusual phenomena such as new mountain ranges rising up in just hours, rivers flowing backwards, and tsunamis causing oceans to flow over large land areas. Massive waves made the seas almost impossible to navigate, and airport runways were breaking up from the heaving up and down with every new earthquake, making it extremely difficult for planes to take off or land.

TV news programs were filled with videos of landslides, swaying bridges, toppled buildings, downed forests of trees, and raging fires caused by broken gas lines. Big cracks in the ground were swallowing up everything in their path, and zoo animals were running loose due to collapsed cages. Panic was reaching a peak as people began to fear the very ground beneath their feet would give way. There seemed to be no safe place anywhere. There was no longer any doubt about what was happening or what was causing it. The Earth was close to being in its final throes.

Blakeley and her team in the NSA lab were feverishly trying to break the code. It was proving to be especially difficult because even though they were sure the data was formatted in the universal computer math of binary ones and zeros, interpreting the results of some alien language may not be possible. Their best hope was to have their computing algorithms look for repeating patterns and try to assign alphanumeric values to them. Without quantum computing, this would all be a wasted effort. Even so, the computers ground away on the data for hours with no results.

As more and more of Kristof's data scrolled across her screen, Blakeley began to notice the background communication only took place several minutes after the latest quake and only lasted for a short period of time. She suspected that, after creating an earthquake, the capsules waited for some length of time and then took a reading to see if the Earth had gone into resonance. If not, they would make contact and create another quake at an increase in magnitude. She was convinced the transmission was initiated by the capsule located in the Antarctic. If they could somehow block that communication, the capsules may leave their positions and fly up to an altitude where they have line-of-site over the curvature of the Earth and attempt to re-establish communication.

She had become very familiar with the transmission properties, so calculating a phase canceling frequency that would block the communication wouldn't be too difficult. Delivering it would be a different story.

She Skyped Sara to find out if Kristof thought it might work and if he had the necessary equipment. He sat with a blank stare for a couple of minutes and then told Sara he was sure it would work, but the equipment he needed was all back in Serbia. It would have to be transported near the Vostok station. This new development meant another round of negotiations with the Russians, which wasn't near as heated. They even agreed to lend some equipment and manpower, if needed. As soon as this agreement was reached, Kristof told Sara how to contact his technicians and gave her a list of the things they would need to bring to the Antarctic. He would contact them with instructions once they got there.

Also needed would be an oil rigging crew to drill a six-inch hole a couple thousand yards into the ice near where the capsule was thought to be located. The techs would insert a frequency cable down the shaft for Blakeley's canceling signal. Sara handed this task off to Ryan, and it didn't take him long to find a crew willing to go immediately. Kristof started working on the program he would use to fire the phase canceling frequency.

Unfortunately, the landing strip at Vostok could only accommodate relatively small, light planes due to thin ice at this time of year. It would take several flights to get Kristof's techs and the drilling crew with all their equipment transported there. The Russians, as negotiated, assisted in the landings and made all their vehicles available for the trek across the ice. The crews would make their way to the center of the search area and set up their equipment.

They weren't expecting to actually find the spot where the capsule broke through the ice, but what Kristof had calculated was good enough. The weather conditions weren't bad, and the rigging crew didn't think drilling into the ice would be too difficult or take very long. While the shaft was being drilled, a temporary shelter would be set up for Kristof's equipment. His plan, if it could all get set up and functioning in time, was to wait for the communication to start after the next earthquake and immediately trigger the cancellation frequency. Waiting until it started would keep the capsules from detecting it ahead of time. Everyone in the lab was aware of his plan and were, much to their own disbelief, anxiously awaiting the next quake.

Like most other structures in the world, the lab itself had sustained some severe damage. Sara could see fallen trees along with dust and smoke in the air outside the window. There was a rumbling sound with every quake, and the Earth had been vibrating long after the last one stopped, making everyone think it could be getting very close to resonance. It may take only a few more attempts for the capsules to put Earth into the 'shake of death.'

CHAPTER 20
THE BATTLE

The US military had plans to bomb the capsules as soon as they were located, but if they weren't found soon, they would just carpet bomb the center of the search areas.

The Navy had moved their south sea aircraft carriers as close as possible to the Antarctica coordinates calculated by Kristof's program. All available search planes and some fighters were deployed to the area. Even with the heightened urgency of taking some immediate action, the Russians were still not happy about having US war machines anywhere near Vostok station. The Thule Greenland US Air Force base sent search planes and a few fighter planes to the Greenland site as well.

When Kristof got word the drilling crew and his technicians had completed their work, he immediately tested its functions. When he was satisfied everything worked, he and Sara, like everyone else, awaited the next quake.

It came, right on time, high on the Richter scale, and had everyone in the lab hanging on to something to keep from falling. The lab walls were shaking, pipes were rattling, ceiling tiles were falling, the floor was doing a dance, and everyone had a 'what's next' look on their faces. Then a short time after the peak of this latest tremor had passed, just as Blakeley predicted, the communication pattern showed up.

Kristof immediately sent a command to trigger the phase cancellation signal. Everyone gathered around his screen, holding their breath and desperately hoping for a blank screen. A large sigh of relief was heard when there was no new activity on the screen, but Kristof remained transfixed to the computer screen. When it didn't start up again for several more seconds, he told the general, "There won't be much time to locate and destroy them. They will likely back out of the crust and try to re-establish communication. I won't be able to block that, and if they dive back into new locations, I will never find them again in time."

General Tallmadge ordered all search planes to leave both areas and all fighters not already in the air to take off immediately and find those capsules. He turned back to Kristof and asked, "When we locate them and start attacking, couldn't they just fly away?"

Kristof speculated, "Well I suspect they're programmed to deflect or destroy anything that's a potential threat, including an enemy attack. If I wrote their program, they would never give up."

Alarms went off. Pilots ran onto the decks of the aircraft carriers, got in their fighter planes, and one by one were waved off the deck into the air. Taking off was precarious because the sea was undulating wildly due to the earthquakes. Fighters taking off from the Thule air force base had similar problems as the runway had cracks and were heaving up and down. All shipboard and airborne radar were trained on the areas where the capsules were thought to be located.

As soon as they backed out of their shafts and popped up, their GPS coordinates were relayed to the pilots. It took only minutes for the fighters already in the search area to spot the capsule over Greenland and to get its silhouette on their battle screens. In the lab, everyone's attention shifted to a large flat screen that was displaying split screen video from the fighters at both sites.

One of the fighters in Greenland immediately fired a laser guided missile that struck the capsule, sending it tumbling out of control. This inspired some hope, which quickly dissipated when they saw it recover and rotate its domed end around to face the fighter. The entire surface of the dome began to glow. The glow quickly collapsed into a small circle in the center and a beam of what seemed like pure energy shot out like a laser. When it struck, the fighter was instantly turned into a small vapor cloud. This was totally unexpected. The military had thought once they were located, a couple of missiles would just dispense with them. Now that they had shown such potent offensive capability, it was a whole new ballgame. It was speculated the beam must be what they use to vaporize small cosmic bodies threatening their planet. Now it was vaporizing our fighters.

Several other fighters suffered the same fate until the pilots began to realize it took several seconds for the capsule to charge up another beam, so they had that scant amount of time to take evasive action. This took intense concentration, perfect timing, and a lot of luck, but these were some of the best pilots in the world. They continued firing missiles, which had the capsule constantly rotating toward another fighter, affecting its accuracy. Nonetheless, it was still able to take out several unlucky ones. If the battle continued this way, it would soon be lost.

On the Antarctic end of the planet, the other capsule had been located and a similar battle was taking place. As planes fired missiles, the capsule eliminated many of them with its lethal beam. Martin Caldwell, the shuttle pilot on the Moon mission, was flying one of the fighters and realized they were in serious jeopardy. He radioed Kyle, whose fighter was just off his starboard wing, saying, "If we don't come up with something soon, we're all going to be blasted out of the sky."

Kyle responded, "Copy that."

Martin suggested to Kyle, "If we can get it in somewhat of a crossfire and hit it with two missiles at the same time, we might knock it out of control and possibly do some damage."

Kyle agreed to get to the one o'clock position, and Martin would get to five o'clock. Martin radioed all the other pilots in the area, telling them to keep the capsule busy but stay out of their crossfire. He informed Kyle they would have to get into missile synchronous mode so both of their missiles would hit it at exactly the same instant. He instructed, "Bring up your missile screen, hit sync, select frequency five, and then hit connect."

After a few seconds Kyle radioed, "Done...my screen shows connected."

Martin replied, "Mine too...let's go."

It was a maneuver fraught with danger, but it was desperation time. They both rolled their fighters up and out and skillfully flew to their locations. Martin radioed, "I'm there and locked on."

Kyle responded, "Me too. Give me a count down."

Martin counted, "Three...two...one...FIRE!"

Two laser guided missiles dropped down from their latches under the wings, ignited, and streaked toward the domed end of the capsule. The simultaneous strikes sent it tumbling end over end for thousands of yards, but when it recovered, there was no sign of damage. It rotated toward Kyle's plane and Martin, seeing the dome glowing, yelled over the radio, "Kyle, it's on you. Get out of there." Kyle pushed the stick hard to the right, but it was too late. The beam hit his fuselage, and his entire plane just disappeared. Martin couldn't take even one second to grieve for his friend as he now knew they were going to need a lot more fire power.

While flying around the side of the capsule to avoid its beam, Martin spotted a slight heat trail streaming out of the propulsion end. He knew he couldn't keep the laser locked onto a port that small, but a heat seeking missile would definitely zero in on it. That kind of missile could also be set to explode inside the capsule.

He radioed the aircraft carrier to see if they had any on board. The munitions officer said it's been a while since they had been in service, but he would check with the chief in the ammunition crib. Chief Daniels, who had a sleeve full of longevity stripes, answered, "I do have some, but I'll have to check if they're still operational. If so, I'll equip some fighters and get them airborne as fast as possible."

Back over Greenland, many of the fighters returned to base because they were out of missiles. The squadron commander, Jim Sanders, radioed the Thule airfield to send replacements. With most of his squadron destroyed, he found himself almost alone with the capsule. If he didn't get help soon with this seemingly impossible to win battle, he was going to have to make a difficult decision about himself and the few other remaining fighters. For now he told them to just spread out and keep firing missiles to at least keep the capsule occupied.

After he fired his next missile, the capsule rotated toward him and, while taking evasive action, he spotted a small squadron of fighters coming in from the north. It's too soon to be the replacements and he didn't immediately recognize their profile. He got the silhouette of one of them on his battle screen and called out, "Computer identify." Seconds later the computer displayed Russian SU-27 long-range air defense crafts, six 27R air-to-air missiles and two R-73E advanced air-to-air missiles. He radioed this information to general Tallmadge who told him he was in contact with the Russian squadron leader and they're friendly.

Jim didn't think they would fare any better than his fellow pilots but was glad to have more fighters around to keep him from being one of the only targets left for the capsule to zero in on, and they may buy some precious time.

When the Russian planes got close, one fighter peeled off from the formation and headed for the capsule. Not knowing how lethal it was, he continued to head straight for it even as its dome began to glow. The American pilots couldn't warn him, and before he could get off a missile, the beam took him out. The other Russian pilots now held back to see how the Americans were dealing with it. Once they learned about the few seconds delay it took to build up a new beam, they joined in firing missiles and performing evasive maneuvers. Still, things were looking bleak. One of the Russian fighters had just the very tip of his wing struck by the beam and spun out of control. He was able to get it somewhat stabilized but was out of the fight.

Back in the lab, frustration had gripped everyone as it was out of their hands, and all they could do was watch the split screen. An air force colonel hurriedly approached the general telling him, "Sir, I had thought our fighters would take care of the capsules as soon as they were located. Now that that's in serious doubt, I kind of feel justified in revealing some top-secret information."

The general barked, "For God's sake man, give me anything you've got!"

The colonel revealed, "I've heard rumors about some kind of ultrasonic stealth drone being developed, but it's a highest-level, top-secret project. It's supposed to fire some kind of charged particle beam and travel at an incredible speed. I don't know if it's even off the drawing board...."

By now the general had stopped listening to him and turned to his headset wearing adjutant and ordered, "Get me the secretary of the air force in Washington!"

Within minutes the general had talked to the secretary who gave him the name and contact information for the engineer in charge of the project.

The adjutant said, "I have the engineer on the phone, sir."

The general started by yelling, "Whatever kind of weapon you have has to—"

The engineer interrupted him saying, "We have the video feed from your fighters and have been monitoring the situation. When it became apparent we didn't have the fire power to deal with them, my entire crew went to work and got Ultra-1 in the air. We have an Ultra-2, but it's not air worthy at all. Since we're closer to Greenland than the Antarctic, I started it in that direction.

"It's designed to be the fastest stratospheric capable vehicle ever and carry the most powerful weapon of any airborne fighter but has never been tested anywhere near those limits. It should exceed the speed of the X-43, which reaches Mach 9.6 or 7,307 miles per hour, and depending on the atmosphere conditions, Ultra-1 could be there in ten to fifteen minutes. When you give me the capsule's coordinates, I'll get back with a more exact arrival time.

"Your fighters can keep it busy until Ultra-1 arrives, but as soon as they spot it, they'll have to get at least five miles away to avoid the shock wave, assuming there's going to be a shock wave."

The general gave him the coordinates and then immediately called Jim Sanders to bring him up to date. In less than a minute, the adjutant reported that, "Ultra-1's time of arrival at the Greenland site is eleven minutes, sir." The general told him to warn the Russian pilots to leave the instant the American fighters do but don't reveal the reason.

Ryan approached the general and asked, "Do you have something that might help?"

The general said, "The air force has this large, ultrasonic drone thing that fires some kind of high-powered beam. They're not even sure it's going to work, but it may be better than what we've got. It's supposed to be top secret, but right now I don't care who finds out about it."

During all this time, the vibration hadn't stopped from the most recent quake, and now a constant low frequency rumbling sound could be heard. The lights and flat screen in the lab were flickering, as if the power was threatening to go out. It was going to be a long eleven minutes.

The pilots at both ends of the globe continued to fight a losing battle when Jim Sanders in Greenland spotted something strange just starting to leave a vapor trail while streaking in from the south. It was just a dot in the sky that didn't appear on his radar screen. It couldn't be the reinforcements from the base because with a vapor trail, it had to be at a very high altitude. This must be the secret weapon dropping down from the upper atmosphere. He immediately ordered all his fighters to get at least five miles out of the area. The Russians obediently followed.

While streaking away, he got an eerie feeling because being ultrasonic it had to be slowing down from the speed of sound, but there was no sonic boom. Once out of range, Jim and his group oriented their planes so they could still get the silhouette of the capsule on their battle screens and maybe get a glimpse of Ultra-1 in action. Suddenly there was a blinding light in the sky and a deafening explosion sound. It was as if a million lightning bolts and thunderclaps struck all at once.

In the lab, the Greenland display on the flat screen went all white. The fighter pilots were temporarily flying blind until the light finally faded and their eyes readjusted. When they looked back at their battle screens, the capsule's silhouette was gone and there was nothing else to be seen in the area. Jim radioed General Tallmadge to find out what happened. The general told him that the planet killer had been dispatched and Ultra-1 had left the area.

The battle here was over, so the Russian planes immediately headed back to the north. They couldn't have gotten much of a look at Ultra-1, but they certainly saw its capability. The American pilots breathed a big sigh of relief and headed back to their bases.

The general was about to order Ultra-1 to Antarctica when Martin Caldwell reported the capsule they had been battling was gone. As it flew away, they had attempted to follow, but it sped up and a sphere of rainbow-like colors developed around it. There was a flash of light, along with a slight trail of something like mist, and it was no longer there. The general, figuring the capsules must only work in tandem, ordered Martin and his crew to stand down.

When he announced these events in the lab, the celebration that erupted was like the locker room exuberance of a team that had just won the Super Bowl. During the celebration, Sara was definitely the center of attention because everyone knew that without her discovery of the killers' communication, the Earth would probably be on the way to oblivion. After high fives and hugs all around, Sara had a short thank you conversation with Blakeley. Then she, Ryan, and Kristof took off their headsets and walked out the front door, exhausted from the long ordeal.

There was earthquake damage as far as they could see. The shuttle had partially fallen into a crack in the runway. The crane used to bring the capsule into the lab was laying on its side. Some of the buildings on the base had suffered severe damage, but others had come through mostly unscathed. They stood in silence, taking it all in, for a few minutes when Kristof, in his Serbian accent, said, "Looks like Uncle Nikola was right."

There was some concern the capsule that got away might return someday, but for now, the crisis was over, and life slowly drifted back to normal. In time, Mother Nature and man would massage the worst of the damage back into a habitable condition, but the scars would be a long-time reminder of just how fragile our existence can be.

After the frenzy of the last couple of years, Ryan and Sara settled back into their usual routines, hoping for a more quiet, simple life in their future. Ryan began to have doubts though when, one evening just after dark, he heard Sara yell, "Rachel, are you still outside glued to my old telescope?"

THE END (maybe)

www.ingramcontent.com/pod-product-compliance
Lightning Source LLC
LaVergne TN
LVHW010111170826
845678LV00012B/2356
9798889253785